The Warrior Mystic in Viet Nam

Volume 1

A Tree by the River

a novel by

James Lloyd Dunn

Blue Forge Press

Port Orchard ✿ Washington

A Tree by the River
Copyright 2018
by James Lloyd Dunn

First eBook Edition
November 2018

First Print Edition
November 2018

For information about film, reprint or other subsidiary rights, contact: blueforgegroup@gmail.com

Blue Forge Press
7419 Ebbert Drive Southeast
Port Orchard, Washington 98367
360.550.2071 ph.txt

Acknowledgements

I would like to thank the folks who inspired me, hounded me a little, and insisted that I publish A Tree by the River, beginning with my wife Sally, our three children, and Lou Goldine, who read the earliest writings and urged me to continue. I would be remiss if I didn't also thank Donna Anderson, Scot Wilcox and everyone who encouraged me to "keep on keeping on."

The Warrior Mystic in Viet Nam

Volume 1

A Tree by

the River

a novel by

James Lloyd Dunn

Chapter 1

The politicians called it Vietnamization. Most of us here in this country call it insanity. But orders are orders, and so we all go through the motions of trying to train our South Vietnamese counterparts on the finer points of warfare. The problem is our reconnaissance training took twenty-six weeks. Our South Vietnamese friends will be lucky if theirs lasts six. Add to that the idea that in the daytime, they are our friends. And at night they hate us, shoot at us, and wish only to be left alone to manage their affairs.

Most of the men on the ground, artillery, infantry and

air guys know the reality of the situation. But politicians are so sure they have it all figured out from their comfy offices in D.C. The truth is that America is abandoning its' ally. We all know it. And so do they. The latest irony in this most ironic war is that their cooks are cooking in our mess halls, and us Americans are "guests" at our own camps.

I'm sitting with some of the guys and enjoying a mid-day meal of beans, rice, and some type of meat in the mess-hall. All the guys are raving about the shish-ka-bobs that the newest Vietnamese chef has cooked up.

From behind me I hear the voice of a guy I thought was already on his way home. "Hey Toby, you're supposed to get your ass down to the CO's! Seems like some shot-down flyboy is hiding out by the river, and the Major wants to know if you want to lead the rescue party."

I turn around and spot the speaker. Sure as hell it IS McDuff! "I thought you were taking the chopper out tonight. Heard you couldn't wait to get back to momma and the kid."

McDuff grins and rubs his chin, "Yeah, well, I told Major that I'd ride along on the condition that you're team leader." He rubbed his freckled hand through his short, sandy hair. His face had the magical ability to defy the hot sun of Viet Nam and maintain its ghostly white complexion as a startling background for all those bright orange freckles that covered his face.

I sigh, staring at him. "Four more days for most of us, but we almost have to try getting the pilot out, but you...You could be gone today. Shouldn't you be out there on the helipad?"

A goofy grin spreads across his face, "Me? And miss all the fun? You better get into the Major's office if you want to lead the pick-up team." The Major nods when I pull the tent flap aside. His rugged face shows a lot of mileage, though he's probably only in his mid-thirties. He's a warrior and a mustang who'd started as an enlisted grunt. Exactly my kind of CO.

Without preamble he spoke, "I know you're real short on time in country, and I wouldn't blame you if you passed, but I'm not sure ARVN is up to this one."

I shudder at the entire mess. We needed at least six more months to get the locals up to speed, but the way things were going, in no time they'll be on their own, and definitely lost.

Furrowing his brow, he continues, "It bothers the hell out of me that we're running out on the ARVN troops, but we just can't leave one of our own flyers..."

"Did it happen? The Treaty?"

The Major nodded. "Kissinger signed it, the North signed it, and so the South really has no choice."

All of us had listened to the news, gathered around a desk in the mess. Congress was getting ready to pull all the funding for the war. Americans were getting just plain sick and tired of this part of the world.

"So, not just some of us, but all of us out by April?"

He nodded. "But today we've got a downed airman. Want to take a team and find him, or not?"

"Couldn't live with myself if I went home knowing an American flyboy got left behind just because I was down to four days."

"Good!" The Major slapped a topographical map and then pointed to a line representing a river. "He's real close to us, right here somewhere...and here's your drop zone." He glanced at his watch. "Shit! I've got orders to get my ass to Saigon ASAP. Guess I'll be taking McDuff's chair on the mail plane."

"So who does the briefing, me?"

"Lieutenant Holden will do the briefing. Pick your team and be back here in thirty minutes."

I did something I don't normally do. I came to full and proper attention, and saluted the Major. "It's been an honor having you as CO, sir. You're ten times better than the guy you replaced."

"Thanks for the glowing assessment, but it's time for a shift change." He glanced towards the tent flap. "I'm hoping you'll treat this new guy with the same respect. Right now I have to catch a hop to Saigon. My wife and I bought a home in Lawton, near Fort Sill, and I'm eager to see it."

"Paul's Valley isn't that far from Lawton, sir. Maybe I'll look you up when I get back."

The Major nodded, grabbed and slung a nearby duffel bag across his back, "By the way, as usual, the brass wants you to do your best to avoid engaging the enemy."

"Roger that, sir. If I never see another black pajama hombre, I'll die a happy man."

He turned and headed to the area where the mail chopper sat with its huge props idling lazily. I watched him scrunch down with that duffle bag on his shoulder and scoot under the blades. Then and there I decided all officers aren't assholes, just the majority of them. But his replacement, Lieutenant Holden, is for sure.

I went back to the mess to gather my team. When we got to the CO's tent, that short and chubby Second Lieutenant was staring at a map on the chart table.

"The pilot is here, we get dropped here! We'll have to hump it the last eleven clicks from the drop zone..." his nasal voice conjured memories of fingernails on blackboards.

I wanted to go, not talk, and the CO usually let me brief the team and pick the landing zone. So I spoke up. "Pardon the interruption, sir, but I have two questions. One is why can't we land here, and cut the hike in half?"

Lieutenant Holden seemed to puff up to try to make him look taller than he was. I was sure he was going to stand on his tippy-toes, but he didn't. "The last officer's briefing showed us that the zone," his chubby finger swept the map along the river, "is heavily infiltrated. So what is your second concern, Sergeant?"

"Why do you keep saying *we*?"

The Lieutenant stretched up as much as his fat little frame would allow, which might have been five feet six in thick heels. "This is my mission, Sergeant, and I'll lead it by the book."

I glanced at the team, and the disgust on their faces was almost funny. The Lieutenant failed to notice.

"I just came from the Major's tent, sir, and I was given the mission. Tradition in country says that officers stay in camp. Recon teams are run by the NCO's."

The Lieutenant glanced out the tent flap and watched as the Huey to Saigon lifted off. "This isn't a Recon job. It's a rescue. And with the Major on that chopper, it looks like I'm the ranking officer in this unit."

I couldn't believe this arrogant, ignorant green-ass dweeb. I was wondering if I'd face a court-martial if I told him he could have my seat, but before I could open my mouth McDuff spoke.

"With due respect *sir*! If you insist on leading this mission, sir, you'll end up with a load of gooks. There's not a man here who would *volunteer* to follow you into the boonies, sir!"

What I didn't need my last week in country was a mutiny, or a court-martial. I raised my hand, and the men were instantly silent. The Lieutenant looked at me. "Sir, this is a totally voluntary mission. All of us are short timers."

"What the hell happened to chain of command?" His voice went nearly an octave higher.

"Reconnaissance Patrols are usually made up of enlisted men, with an NCO in charge."

His face went purple with rage.

I nodded in the direction of the ARVN command tent. "Maybe the locals wouldn't mind if you rode with them."

"Damn it!" he pounded his fist on the map. "You all know I just got in country. If I just sit here in camp I won't see any action at all!"

Miller had quietly stepped outside and was using the radio to try to raise the Major. He shook his head at me. "Can't raise anyone, must be in a blackout." he said softly. The other guys looked to me.

The best I could come up with was, "It'll only be a six hour mission, sir. You'll have plenty of other chances to see some action."

"I go, or the mission is off!" He puffed up and tried to stare me down and then growled, "I am the ranking officer on the post. That's final! That's how it'll be!"

I looked at the men. For the same reason as the other guys, I wanted a chance to grab that Navy Pilot. Most of us had our asses saved by flyboys before.

There was a long silence as each man waited to see how this was going to go down.

Smitty's voice came from the back of the room. "Here's an idea. The Lieutenant goes as an observer, but Sergeant Allman's the team leader."

"I'm in," says Miller.

McDuff steps forward one step. "Me too!"

Three more stepped forward. I looked at the Lieutenant.

"Shit! Since when do the enlisted men run the army?"

McDuff looked maliciously at the Lieutenant. "It's the only way I'll volunteer, sir!"

The Lieutenant glares at me.

"I'm fine with you as an observer, but it's my show, or it's a no go, sir." I was still wondering if we'd all be busted for insubordination or maybe even treason.

The Lieutenant exhaled. "Whatever! As long as I'm on that chopper."

McDuff grabs my arm as we headed out and whispers, "Maybe that asshole will accidentally step in front of a stray bullet. I'd be happy to arrange it."

I shake my head. "Too much paperwork. If we shoot anybody, we shoot Charlie. The Major said avoid any contact if at all possible."

McDuff shrugs and smiles. I come close to telling him to stay in camp, but I know I need his ears and eyes.

So we load up and go airborne, but the mood is not right at all.

I usually try to nap on the longer trips, and the "pop-pop-popping" of the chopper's blades normally lulls me to sleep. But, not this trip.

I'm Staff Sergeant Toby Allman, and a veteran on

more than 50 Long Range Reconnaissance Patrols, but today our task is literally to find a needle in a haystack. So off we go... one slim chance to save the life of a bad luck fly-boy shot down in the closing days of a bad luck war. And me in charge of a squad that wants to cap an officer who's looking for a medal. It just don't get any better than this.

I decide to get my head into the game ASAP. Find this pilot and get him home without casualties. The flyboy's position was triangulated to be on or near the infamous Ho Chi Minh Trail, which isn't really a single trail but a whole network of interconnecting paths and roads all through the border area between Viet Nam, Laos and Cambodia.

Technically his position might be in Laos, and that's a no-go zone for us. But the powers that be have decided it would be in bad taste to abandon a fly-boy anywhere in these final days. So naturally, we get tasked to go find him.

Normally, borders are a big deal, but one side of a river is Laos, which is a no-go land. Wade about thirty feet though, and it's all cool. But when an American warrior gets in a jam, borders don't mean squat.

Besides, there's been some recent intel indicating major enemy movements all through this area, and someone higher up has modified the operation so that we get to be dropped in a "secure" zone, and then we get to hump through to an "unsecured" area.

"Unsecured" is military double talk for enemy positions. The flyboy's last message has been the sightings of a heavy troop movement right under his treetop perch.

I glance at the team, mostly guys I've fought beside and learned to love and trust. There's Miller, a tall, skinny, black kid from Detroit who has only been in country five months, but as professional as any. He is our radioman, and a crack marksman who had a special knack for killing VC tree snipers, and he has five notches on his CAR-15 stock to prove it.

Next to him is Smitty, fresh from the not-so-mean streets of Des Moines, but a heads-up guy with an uncanny ESP-like ability to smell trouble. McDuff is a string-bean kid from Tennessee who can shoot the left eye out of a rat at 300 meters, and serves as our official resident sniper. He earns good beer money by snookering other soldiers into shooting contests.

I still have Hardy, my munitions man, and Dillard. Both of them are great soldiers and good guys who are true professionals. Hardy is toting the ditty bag with all the claymore mines and booby-traps, while Dillard is an expert on setting trip-wire traps in the unlikely event we'll spend the night in the field.

The only fly in my ointment is that dip-shit Second-Lieutenant who got to camp last week, fresh out of OCS. He got under everyone's skin right away by spending most of his time crying that there was not going to be much war left to fight and it was just his luck to miss all the action.

And of course, there's McDuff, who wants to cap said Lieutenant.

Miller caught my eye, and tapped his chest pocket while raising his eyebrows rapidly. Inside a Huey, talk is minimal because it's not exactly a quiet place, so we use sign language. He's asking me if I have my baby bible in my chest jacket pocket. I smile and use the thumb and index fingers of my left hand to lift the battered black book to reassure him. I'm not particularly religious, having confined my church visits to Easter, Christmas, and the occasional wedding, but most of us have amulets of some kind, a rabbit's foot, or a lucky picture we carry. The little black bible is my amulet.

My mom made me promise to keep it with me twenty-four-seven, and being a veteran of too many Patrols without a scratch makes me think it may indeed protect me, since I'm something of a legend around here. So I'm not about to piss off the Goddess of Luck on my last mission.

On paper, the plan is simple. We go low, jump out, and hump about eleven clicks to a river, find the flyboy in a tree and call in another chopper. But there's no guarantee that we won't get ambushed at the drop site, or even find the pilot. Plus, we have no clue if it'll be too hot a zone to get a chopper to the pick point.

Outside of that, it's your normal mission. Come to think about it, not one of my fifty-six missions would have been described as normal.

The chopper lurches down hot and fast, and we bail out on the first pass. Barely eight seconds later, the seven of us fanned out in a defensive circle. Only six of us actually fan out, because the Lieutenant manages to twist his ankle getting out, so he's softly howling and hanging back. As ranking NCO I guess I'll be writing his Purple Heart report.

Worse thing is he'll be slowing the whole team down, but since the Huey's long gone before we know about the ankle issue, we are down to just two choices. Leave him here and make haste to the river, or let him slow us down and get there later.

McDuff smiles, winks, and raises his hand like a school kid. "Sergeant," he says sarcastically, "I'll be glad to stay here with the Lieutenant. You guys can go on ahead. The chopper can pick us up on the way back."

I scowl darkly, "We stay together... I'll be point. Dillard, you'll cover the rear."

There is a theory in the Rangers that says that the sooner a mission goes screwy, the better it'll be in the long run. So I'm actually a little bit glad this green asshole tweaked his foot. Maybe it's the total of our bad luck. Maybe in the grand scheme of things, he is only along so he could go home with a medal, even if it is just a purple heart.

Eleven kilometers is just over six miles. In a perfect world, without enemy snipers, snakes, booby-traps and the Murphy factor, that would take the squad around thirty to forty minutes.

But Rangers aren't trained to operate in a perfect world, so we set out, knowing only that the dip-shit

Lieutenant is going to slow us down. The jungle here is light to moderate overgrowth, and recent rains make it easy to see any tracks of enemy movements. And there aren't any tracks. But we still have to be careful and guard against ambushes.

We get to the river in the early afternoon. The squad fans out at the edge. I lay prone at a break in the trees and take my time studying the opposite shore for movement, traps, and possible crossing points.

Recent rains turned the river to muddy brown, but it's moving at a pretty good clip. I've no idea how deep it is. But right here it's only about thirty or forty feet across, which is a good thing.

So if I were a VC sniper, I'd be sitting in a tree and waiting till the lead guy was across, and he'd signaled the others into the river, then I'd blast the whole squad.

I know the drill, but so does my enemy, so I take extra time and care studying the trees on the opposite bank. Most of the nearby ones are what the guys called monkey trees, weird misshapen trees with sharp pointy branches that make climbing dangerous. The VC use monkey tree branches to make pit-traps on a trail that impale any unsuspecting bastard with the bad luck to fall in. To make it more fun they put some of their own shit on each pointed branch, figuring that a wounded and an infected soldier is better than a dead one.

Just because monkey trees are nasty trees doesn't

guarantee that Charlie won't scramble up one anyway and set up an ambush. Hell, even the pilot might have managed to hide in one of them.

So I take my time. I watch and listen to the birds and ever-present monkeys until I am convinced that there's absolutely no danger lurking on the opposite bank. That's a sign the river's safe to cross.

But the dense jungles of neighboring Laos, just across that small meadow are an entirely different animal. All of it has the potential to hide an ambush, a flyboy, or both or nothing.

The monkeys and the birds let me know that there's nothing close enough to scare them, so I take a deep breath and step into the river. The water is warm and muddy, and the bottom is a little bit soft.

A couple of steps and I'm only up to my knees, and so I squat lower. My heart is playing a tattoo rhythm, and I have to consciously force myself to breathe.

The most dangerous part of any patrol is a river crossing because there's no cover and no way to avoid presenting a first-class target. I hunker down lower, trying to make less of a profile, my shirt soaked up to the middle of my belly.

The heat plus the fear factor bring large drops of sweat to my forehead. Salt is pouring into my eyes and it burns like hell. Sweat drips down my nose and cheeks to drop into the river.

The plopping noise sounds loud enough to wake up even a snoring sniper.

The middle of the river isn't all that deep, but the fast current worries me. So I shorten my steps and spread my stance to get me finally to the other side.

I glance back for the team, and note that my first visual sweep doesn't find anyone. McDuff, my second in charge, is great at hide and peek. It takes two sweeps before I finally spot him, with that lieutenant sticking out next to him looking scared shitless. McDuff rolls his eyes and smiles his shit-eating grin, then squints and nearly disappears. Maybe he's coaching the dumb lieutenant, who is suddenly harder to spot.

I lightly touch my chest, reassuring myself that my small Bible is there. The climb up a slippery muddy slope on the opposite shore takes some time but I manage to stay on my feet long enough to feel the hard ground and ease myself forward into a prone position. I calm my breath as I sweep the area in front.

Has the jungle suddenly gone quiet? I slither up behind a fallen tree branch and check the jungle, looking for anything out of the ordinary.

It's hot enough that steam rises from my shirtsleeves right in front of my eyes, blurring my vision. The afternoon sun can suck up all moisture in less than a minute.

I force my mind to stay in the present. According to the map, there is one sharp turn in the river around here, so this has got to be the area where the pilot is down.

Can he spot me? Is he afraid to contact me for fear

of giving away his position? Is he even around? Shit!

I belly-crawl through the tall grass towards the tree canopy, stopping every couple of feet to sweep the trees with my eyes and my weapon for any sign of company. Former First Sergeant Stevens used to tell me, "This is a war of patience. He who hurries goes home in a body bag."

After convincing myself that there's probably no sniper sighting down on me, I crawl ever so slowly the last fifteen feet to the deeper cover of the jungle. Out of breath from holding my breath I rest near a large gnarled tree.

Then I stop my breath and listen again, allowing my eyes to refocus to help me pick up any tiny movements. But I'm worried. It's not normal to go from normal jungle noises to total silence.

God, I wish I just could stand up and call out for the pilot. Is this sudden silence only because I'm here? Or because I'm not alone?

I crank my head around again back across the river, and spot Miller, McDuff and the guys. Miller raises his eye-brows, and I shrug ever so slightly.

Returning my gaze to the jungle canopy, I search again for any kind of movement, any sudden motion or a darkened shadow that doesn't belong. I check for broken twigs or bent grass that might signal human presence.

Nothing.

But still I wait. What's with the sudden silence? It can't be me.

Something causes my attention to shift to the right, towards the thickest part of the jungle. Was it a sound? A movement? A premonition? Although my eyes dart quickly, my head turns ever so slowly in that direction.

Sergeant Stevens, who taught me all the finer points of patrol, taught that sometimes peripheral vision can see stuff that might be missed by looking directly. Stevens had been always preaching, always teaching, and I owe my life to his lessons.

But all that knowledge didn't keep him from going home in a body bag.

To be fair, Stevens survived all the patrols just fine. He was in his bunk sleeping off a weekend of drinking when Charlie lobbed a mortar round into the base-camp. Stevens was the only casualty.

Funny, Stevens always bragged that he'd die in his sleep. I guess he just figured he'd be an older guy when it happened.

I sit still as a statue for a few more minutes, dead certain that something isn't right. Then a distinct "snap" sounds, and I raise my left hand and turn slowly towards Miller.

He is all white eye-balls. Slowly, I make the fingers walking and pointed to my right. He nods and gets on the radio, so I concentrate on the problem of staying alive.

A louder snap right near me stops my breath. Way too close! I start to raise the CAR-15, but decide on less noise and pull my K-bar. This beautiful black knife is for times when the noise of a shot might not be so smart.

I can smell Charlie now! A potent mixture of garlic and sweat tells me that this isn't a Navy pilot. I slowly release my breath, and still my mind.

From out of the deep shadows a small boy, probably not even yet fourteen appears. He is so close, I'm thinking he'll step on me, but his eyes are focused on the distant bank of the river.

So I let him glide past me. Then I rise up right behind him. I grab his mouth with my left hand. At the same instant I jam that long black blade up underneath his ribs from the back, sawing viciously up and down, left and right. Blood gushes out of his back, soaking my knife, my hand, and most of my arm.

I feel him shudder. He's trying like hell to scream, but my hand's tight on his mouth so all that happens is a muffled grunt. I catch him as his legs turn to rubber and aim him off the trail and into deeper underbrush.

He shits his black pants just as his torso reaches the ground. It's a good, clean kill…except for the huge pool of blood and the shit-stench. Can't do it without the blood, and they always shit their pants. Still, it was way better than a gunshot.

Ah well, so much for avoiding contact with the enemy.

I jerk the K-bar from his back and wipe it on his pant leg. Hearing more sounds off to the right, I look;

check the position of the body. Not good!

Grabbing his black pajamas, I lift and fling him deeper into the jungle. He's only maybe seventy pounds, and goes further than I thought, making a crashing noise that seems loud enough to get a whole regiment's attention.

"Damn!" I whisper, as I slink back into the shadows of heavy greenery. I know I'm supposed to search the body. But not now! More sounds!

I freeze about two meters off the path and in the foliage just as an entire column of VC appears. It's not the best cover ever, but it's what I got.

I slow my breath and avert my eyes from looking directly at a column of grim soldiers marching single file. Each one has a weapon in the ready position. What's odd is only one or two of them have backpacks. They walk right past me with their eyes glued to the far bank of the river. Silently I count them as they pad past.

I quit counting at thirty, knowing this is not going to be my best day. Luckily, the jungle smells so much of rotting life that nobody notices the shit smell from the point man.

They make almost no sound as they move past me, going fast like they have a lot of ground to cover. There's no talk, no heavy breathing either. They don't even pause at the water, but slog across exactly toward the place where Miller and the others are or were. I sure hope the guys have vacated their positions, but I've got too much on my plate to even dare a look.

I inch the barrel of my CAR-15 upwards and train it on the column. If it's my day to die, I'm not going there alone.

I'm almost ready to pull the trigger when a coughing noise makes my head snap back in the direction of the enemy.

About 30 feet down the trail a really tall guy in light brown khakis and a pith helmet who is standing and having a smoke. The guy next to him must be a non-smoker because he's hacking into his hand. And at least fifteen guys in black pajamas have stopped beside him. All the rest are lighting up.

I swallow loudly. This is starting to look like a lot more than a company. Maybe it's the beginnings of a whole battalion coming through. That ignorant CO said there might be a couple of squads looking for the pilot.

The tall guy in khakis has his weapon resting in the crook of his arm. He looks more Chinese than Vietnamese, maybe one of the "advisors" we're always hearing about. I hope Miller's called in his artillery strike, even though it'll be ARVN and not American guns these days.

Now the khaki guy's nostrils are starting to flair in and out like maybe he's smelling the shit. His eyes narrow now and he starts searching the close terrain. If he sees me, I've got to swing the barrel around back at him, and all he has to do is raise his weapon. I'm thinking I'm going to lose this one.

And if he sounds an alarm, all hell's going to break loose! Better to just get the hell out of here! I edge backwards, trying to disappear.

A millisecond of a high-pitched scream is all the warning that comes before a monstrous explosion hits right in front of the khaki guy. Shit, any closer and I'd be dead.

So I pull the trigger and the bullets sweep the column in the water from the opposite bank. I'm dragging the barrel to my right to get the ones in the river, and then there is only one remaining on this side. The bam-bam of the weapon lasts just a few seconds, but time seems to slow down to almost nothing as I watch my rounds hitting chests and necks and backs and legs. Each shell pops out blood, and each enemy drops in the water. The river turns from clear to red in front of me. For some strange reason I'm deciding I'll get a drink, up-stream later on.

The last VC has not yet entered the river, and turns back in my direction. I see clearly the smaller size, long hair, and face of a girl, and watch as bullets from my weapon strike her ankle and spin her around. Yet another shell hits her right thigh and still one more, still higher slams into her right shoulder.

A huge, blinding, brilliant-flash of light, a powerful percussive slam, and I'm going airborne. I fly high towards the river like a kite in a windstorm, directly into one of those damned monkey trees.

I watch in a detached slo-mo way as the tree gets closer and closer. I hear a prolonged scream, and I know my mouth is open. But that better not be me!

By the grace of God, the branches soften my flight and slam me into the trunk of the tree.

I have willed myself to turn away, thinking that if I don't see that damn tree it won't hurt as much. My weapon slips from my grip. I lurch to grab for it but miss, and watch as it cartwheels away in graceful slow motion.

I slam into the tree back first, knocking the wind out of me. I gasp, and gasp, and bite the air until finally I'm able to pull gulps of air into my lungs. I must be seven or eight feet up in the damned tree.

I look down to my mid-section and see a tree branch sticking through my lower left belly. I try to wriggle free, but stop instead to stare at the piece of clean white wood sticking out of the left side about six inches. If it went through my belly, why isn't it all covered in blood? No sooner is that thought finished and I see that little droplets of blood are starting to ooze around the branch. My eyes follow the blood as first it stains my shirt, then my pants, and finally falls to the floor of the jungle, making an occasional plopping noise in the sudden silence.

I open my mouth and watch a bloody bubble form. Still focused on the branch sticking out of my belly, the bubble pops as I whisper, "I could be in really big trouble."

And then the artillery comes again. One slams right into the middle of the river, causing a huge plume of muddy, bloody water and flying body parts.

The second, third and fourth rounds land on the opposite shore, receding backwards from the riverbank and away from me.

Below me it's mayhem on cue, with men on the other side of the river yelling, weapons firing, and smoke, fire, and debris. And then as quick as it started, it's all over.

Darkness comes fast in the jungle. Jungles don't give a damn about loud explosions or noisy weapons or even dying soldiers. They just carry on being jungles.

And so I watch as the birds come back, and then a few monkeys show up. Soon enough huge black rats scurry out of somewhere and study the scene. They're curious at first, but grow bold and ravenous. Human flesh must be their version of a top sirloin steak.

Big plumes of black smoke, huge craters and two small fires are all that's left to mark a spot on some insignificant plot of land in Southeast Asia where opposing warriors have played out their deadly little game.

I smile at the irony of it all and feel my consciousness slipping away. My memory flips back to a day in my senior year of high-school. I remember my favorite high-school teacher asking the class; "If a tree falls in the forest, and nobody hears it, did it really happen?"

Chapter 2

I went still closer to see if it was the pilot, I must have been very sleepy, because I couldn't keep my eyes open. I remember thinking that the idea that we see our life pass before us before we die was either wrong, or I wasn't yet to that point. So I drew in a deep breath, and relaxed as much as a guy can when he's got a tree branch sticking out his middle. Interesting enough, it didn't really hurt that much. But as a soldier, I had long learned that a chance to sleep is not to be ignored. I decided that being pinned in a tree afforded some safety, and besides I couldn't move, so I might as well relax. I was asleep in an instant.

A soft breeze woke me up in the middle of the

night. The dark sky was filled with stars, and a big white moon was playing peek-a-boo with the horizon of trees. I watched it rise so slowly until it cleared the canopy and bathed the river in an eerie bluish light, enough light so that I could make out the shapes of the bodies in the scene below my tree.

After every patrol, a squad leader has to make a report to the company commander. With the moon full like it is, and plenty of light, it would actually be safer to do the body count now.

I wondered if any of the squad had survived. I hoped they had the sense to make a hasty retreat before the artillery hit, but knew Miller would have been reluctant to leave me on the other side of the river. He knew the procedures, and the rules called for him to save any part of the squad he could, even if it meant leaving me.

I glanced again at the tree branch sticking out of my middle and tried to move. I could move my hands and neck and head, but my feet just hung there. My body didn't seem to have any feeling. Too bad, I thought. I really wanted to get the body count out of the way while I still had the light of the moon.

Almost as soon as that thought had completely formed, I felt myself floating across the river. I was approaching the lifeless forms along the river, and floated closer to see if any of them were my squad.

The body of a young VC man caught my

attention. He was flat on his back, his eyes looking towards the stars, his mouth wide open. There were five wounds in a well-spaced pattern across his chest and shoulder. I moved past him to the other shore. More VC, and more death. Black rats were busy stripping chunks of flesh from them. I jerked my hand as if to hit one of the rats, but he didn't notice me or scurry away.

I floated away, drawn to the left by a huge crater and a charred tree stump that still smoldered. Moving closer, I found the lifeless body of Miller, and next to him the Lieutenant. Both looked like they had tried to move around in the crater to get more comfortable. About ten feet farther along was the top half of McDuff, also with an open mouth and eyes staring off into the night.

I reached out to close his eyes and was startled to see my hand pass right through him. I tried again, but again my hand and his face couldn't make contact. I held my breath and eased closer, feeling the distance closing. But still there was no contact, no feeling at all as my finger seemed to go right inside his skull. What the hell? I jerked my hand away and tried to mentally process this. Nothing came to mind.

I had to get an accurate count of the dead and wounded. My Company Commander was adamant about these things. So I recounted the dead for our side and theirs. Nothing had changed.

But it would be a heavy-duty report. Five

confirmed Americans and thirteen enemy KIA's.

I floated back across the river but stopped to study the girl. She was maybe twelve or thirteen, a tiny young thing lying next to an AK-47 that was almost as long as she was tall. She breathed in rapid and shallow gasps, and she was staring directly into my eyes. I opened my mouth to tell her I wouldn't hurt her. She narrowed her eyes and opened her mouth and let out a scream that could be heard probably all over the entire country.

The scream shattered the stillness of the night, and I wanted to be gone. I found myself splashing loudly back across the river. On the shore, I lay still to catch my breath, my eyes noticing a tree with a dark blob that was either a huge ape or a human. Maybe it was the downed pilot. I moved closer and squinted at the tree. It was a westerner, probably American, and yet who the hell was here, and if they were friendly, why no help? I moved closer and confirmed it was our team. In fact it looked a lot like me. I went up and grabbed the dog-tags for a better look. "Allman, Toby!"

How in the hell can I be looking directly at me and not be me? The next thing I knew I was closing his eyes, and was startled to see my hand pass right through him. I tried it again, but once again my hand and his face couldn't make contact.

I looked at my hand, flexed the fingers in and out, and carefully tried again to touch Allman's eyelid. I held my breath, and gingerly leaned closer, letting the distance between finger and face diminish. Still there was no sensation of contact, no feeling at all as my finger seemed to go right inside his skull. I jerked my hand away and tried to process this new information. Nothing came to mind.

How could this be happening? How could I be looking at me? The night suddenly got really cold, and I shuddered with a deep sense of tiredness, and felt myself slipping right into the form in the tree.

Now it was me that had the quick, shallow breathe, and the panic in the eyes. What the hell just happened?

I let my eyes wander to the huge crater where the first artillery round hit. A family of huge rats was scurrying in and around the crater, searching for anything edible. One was actually chewing on the pith helmet on the really tall Chinese guy. One of our Vietnamese scouts that we were training had pointed out that those rats would eat anything that had blood on it.

I shuddered and closed my eyes. I needed sleep, but instead of sleeping, my mind went back over the events of the day. Was there something I could have done to make the outcome different? For the longest time no thought at all came to me. Nothing. I drew in a deep breath, and noticed, but hardly cared that I was still blowing frothy red bubbles. The night jungle noises returned, finally lulling me to sleep. I went still closer to see if it was the pilot, moving, and opened my eyes to the sensation of flying down a long dark tunnel. There was no effort, no energy expelled. I was just sort of floating. The speed increased rapidly and lights and sounds flashed by in a roar. It was like riding on a train and passing the objects alongside the tracks. I looked ahead and saw a distant point of light in a field of pitch-black darkness.

Faster and faster I went, and the point of light got bigger and bigger until it nearly consumed me. I remember thinking that this light was a lot brighter than the arc from the welder in shop class in high school. And yet it didn't seem to hurt my eyes.

The walls of the tunnel now glowed, and out of the corners of my eyes I thought I saw movements and strange shapes and voices that made sounds like parts of words. The light in front of me seemed to take on the shape of a man's body, but without any distinct features. I slowed to a stop and stood speechless in front of a shape made out of light.

I had the strange sense of being home, and the figure seemed to open its arms like my mom and dad did when I was a little kid. It absolutely radiated love and warmth, and I felt like I was finally coming back to something or someone I knew I loved so very, very much.

I could feel the love welling up inside of me, and a sensation of completion overwhelmed me. "If this is dying," I thought, "then I'm just fine with it." The light seemed to speak to me wordlessly, like a silent form of mental telepathy or something. As soon as I thought a thought, the light answered. It said, "It is whatever you want it to be, Toby.

It didn't seem strange that I was talking to light, or that the light knew me. In fact it seemed like the most natural thing in the world. I had a feeling that I was reunited with an old friend, or a beloved parent or relative that I couldn't quite remember, but knew I knew and deeply trusted.

"Who are you," I asked. Again the answer came with no sound, no obvious communication. It was like a thought inside my head that just appeared there. It said, "To some I appear as Jesus, or Buddha, or Mohammed. To others I seem like an ancestor, or maybe a parent. What I am called depends upon your belief, but in reality I am the only real part of you. I am yourself."

The love that emanated from this light was so awesome, so immense I felt a strong urge to embrace it. As soon as that thought occurred, the light seemed to encircle me. I was filled with indescribable joy. And confusion. "Then you aren't real?"

The silent answer was instantly in my mind. "I

am the only really real thing in your entire existence. You made up your body, your world, and your games of war. I am the one part of you that is real."

It took me a long time to gather my thoughts, so intense was the feeling of joy and peace and love. But finally my mind formed again around another question, or a lot of questions.

"So I am dead? Did I die? Is this heaven?" The answer that came to me startled me again with its swiftness, and it's content. "Death and dying, heaven and hell are also things you made up. In truth there is only life, not death. Only the is-ness, not heaven and not hell."

"What about the people I killed? I know I have sinned. Thou shalt not kill, right?"

"A more correct statement might be, "Thou cannot kill, and there is only life everlasting."

Now my mind was tumbling, spinning in a vortex of questions that got answers that only led to more questions.

After some time I spoke again, "Can I ask any question I want?"

The light seemed to laugh. There was no meanness, no belittling, just an immense sense of love. "Of course you can ask questions. The whole purpose of your soul's journey is to remember what you tried to forget. That is what your world is for."

I desperately need some answers. "Where am I? If I'm not dead, then what is this? Should I go back? Can I stay here?"

The love that flowed forth from the light was so comforting that a part of me wanted to stay forever, just wrapped in the arms of love. It reminded me of being a little baby, and being held by a parent. But even that didn't approach this.

"You are in a doorway. You have not yet decided to cross the threshold, because there is more you want to do. Nothing that ever happens to you happens without your desire and consent. This is true for you, Toby, and true for all the other parts of yourself that you like to think are other people. In truth it is all you. You are all one. Come and look at this."

The entire background suddenly changed, and became a panoramic view, like a 3-D movie. I saw myself as a light that swooped and entered my mother's womb that grew and became the 'me' that I called 'Toby,' who was a baby, then a toddler, and soon a young child.

Certain moments of my life stood out more sharply, and seemed to draw my attention. I watched myself in 5th grade as Darnell and Bubba Clements dared me to take Billy Watson's lunch money. I saw how much I wanted to fit in with those two, and how I replied, "Watch this."

Then I went over to where Billy was in the line and grabbed him by the collar. He had his money in his shirt pocket, sort of sticking out, and so I just grabbed it. When Billy started crying, I hit him in the eye. I saw all this happen, but I felt Billy's shame and pain and rage. It was as if a boy who looked like a young me was hitting me. The hurt I felt was not so much the physical pain, but the emotional hurt. The embarrassment of giving up my lunch money, of knowing my classmates were watching and laughing.

I watched as the kid that was me went home, and my dad was home from work for some reason when I got there. Maybe Billy's dad told him, or maybe he just had a knack for smelling trouble. He asked me as I laid down my books, "Is there something you need to tell me?" And I knew I couldn't hide it, and so I told him how I'd been dared to take Billy's money. "Did it feel like the right thing when you did it?" I shook my head. "Then undo it," he said.

So I went the next day at lunch hour and sat down beside Billy. I didn't know what to say, so I just handed him the money I took, and mumbled that I was sorry. He smiled through his black eye and said, "Thanks."

Next was me as a teenager driving my Dad's truck. I jammed on the brakes as a group of boys laughed. One kid held a cat by the tail and slammed it into a telephone pole. This time I felt the cat's pain. In fact it was that pain that made me notice the boys. And here was a young me, a skinny sixteen year old, who jumped from the pickup and stopped the boy.

"How would you like it if someone did that to you?" a shrill young voice I recognized as me demanded. All four of the boys were bigger than me, but no one argued. They just backed away. I picked up the stunned cat and cradled it and petted it softly. It relaxed and began to purr. Next I could feel the cat's gratitude. And I knew exactly what was going to happen, because I remembered how the cat scampered away as if nothing happened at all.

Then came a scene from my first patrol. I could see myself trying to hide in the tall grass, fear, choking wet in my throat. That Viet Cong guy was so cautious, so hyper alert. The instant he spotted me and raised his rifle, and it was in that very same instant I squeezed off a round that hit him full in the nose. His head jerked backwards and it actually looked like he jumped.

This time as I watched, I felt his fear turn to stark panic when he spotted me looking thru my sights at him. It was as if I was inside his body, feeling all those emotions, screaming silently as the impact knocked me backwards. The last thought I remembered was a sorrow for a wife and a little daughter never to be seen again. I was amazed that the guy lived as long as he did. I could sense his thoughts of his parents, and his shame that he let his unit down.

One scene melded into another, another patrol

and another kill. In each one I seemed to go inside the mind of my enemy, and die with each one of them. Suddenly it was the present again, or yesterday or whenever ... I was reliving my last patrol.

From a view above the battlefield I could see myself concealed off the trail. But I could also see the boy who was the walking point. This time though, I seemed to go inside that boy's mind as he stepped around what he thought was a rotted log. I got to feel the horror as my hand covered his mouth, and a terrible searing sensation as that black knife entered his back and found his heart.

Wild, delirious fear engulfed me as I relived it all from within the boy's body. Disconnectedness and confusion filled me as I went airborne when the body was being hurled through the underbrush. I felt regret so deep and so painful as the memories of a short life, brothers and a sister, and the comrades were left behind.

The visions and sensations played on an on as I felt the horror and the death of each of the others on that fateful day. "Oh, God" I sobbed. Can the killing ever stop?" As the question was formed in my mind, it was instantly answered with another question. It said. "Can what is eternal ever die?"

The answer stopped my mind. For some time I was totally still, totally without a thought.

I shook my head, trying to clear my thinking. For the longest time my mind could not get words to form in a logical order. Finally I blurted out, "So what does all this mean? Why did I have to watch and feel all that stuff if it didn't happen? Am I having some wild and weird kind of a dream?"

"The experience you see as your life is merely an attempt to forget what your reality is. Whatever happens to you, is to help you to see the truth. You choose the lessons that you need to learn, or more accurately, unlearn... And yes, in a way it is but a dream. Your reality is pure light, pure oneness, and pure love."

I shuddered. "Can the world ever live without wars?"

The answer struck me like a fist in the solar plexus, but not in a physical way. It was just there, within my being with such clarity.

The answer said, "Whatever is in your mind is reflected as your world. If you desire a world of peace, you must begin with a mind at peace."

I knew then that I had to go back. Just a moment earlier I had wished, longed even, to stay here with this incredible being of light. But now I was sure that I had more to do. Instantly I felt myself soaring, roaring backwards down a long vortex tunnel. It seemed so fast that the lights became blurry streaks. I slammed back into my tree perch with a fierce jerk. I forced my eyes to open and beheld the predawn jungle, with the carnage below being methodically cleared by those ravenous black rats.

I wanted to see how bad it was. Instantly, I seemed to rise up and out away from the tree. I floated down the rows of bodies. It all seemed so natural to make the body count again to verify my numbers. Accuracy was something that the brass seemed to holler about a lot. It reassured me when I found the same count as I had made last night.

Again I noted that the girl was still alive, but just barely. She had lost a ton of blood, and I could see it oozing from the bottom of her cotton trousers. Her face showed no pain, no emotion at all. It's as if she had been so conditioned to accepting pain and grief that this was just one more day of the same. I wondered if it might be her last.

A movement off to my left caused me to turn back towards the crumpled bodies on the other side of the river. I blinked and rubbed my eyes and blinked again. A wispy form, almost transparent, seemed to rise up out of each of the bodies. I closed my eyes and counted to three and looked again. Something was still there, moving near each body. My first thought was that another bunch of enemy soldiers was checking on the bodies. But something was not right.

I wished desperately for my weapon, but knew it was out of reach. I looked again at the bodies lying in such a random pattern on the trail. Now I noticed that many of the forms next to the bodies were turning to stare at me. I wanted to be gone, and almost instantly I was floating backwards, and the forms and the bodies receded. I passed again out of the trail and rose up swiftly until I slammed back into my body in the tree.

Now I felt like my own body was suspended in a thick syrup, and every movement took incredible effort. I willed my right hand to come into view, and nearly passed out from the effort, but soon saw it in front of my eyes. My hand appeared solid, not wispy.

What was I seeing then? The memory of those wispy forms was strong, and I was totally unnerved with the idea that they had looked in my direction. None of them had grabbed for a weapon, and none of them seemed surprised to see me. My mind wandered then, back to my encounter with that awesome light. The words were etched in my mind. I remembered the question I had asked, and said it aloud again, "Can the world ever live without wars?" I knew the answer, and I knew that the answer I was given was not about anyone else. I just didn't know what to do with it. So I closed my eyes to sleep.

Chapter 3

aylight and the sound of music pulled me from a sleepless dream. My mind reluctantly came back from deep sleep and remembered my situation. I was still stuck through the middle, and still pinned up about eight feet off the ground in a monkey tree.

So how the hell could I hear music out in the middle of some God forsaken jungle? It sounded off in the distance, but got louder and louder until a band of bald headed monks in orange and brown robes appeared beneath my feet. A tiny old man with wispy white mustache and goatee looked up at my tree and pointed. Behind him was a skinny guy with a tambourine who almost bumped into him. Behind that guy were four more monks. All eyes focused on me.

I wasn't sure whether to wave or call out, so I just watched as the monks huddled up and started a discussion. There were several glances in my direction. The discussion grew animated, with the old guy emphatically repeating himself, and the skinny kid with the tambourine nodding again and again. A chubby guy with a filthy robe and a five o'clock shadow on his shaved head was shaking his head, obviously disagreeing, or at least hoping something he said would carry some weight. Finally the old guy stamped his foot and raised both arms. All the monks instantly stopped talking and looked up at me.

The skinny one stepped directly underneath the tree and asked in broken English, "Do you think you are going to die today?"

"If I don't get out of this tree soon, I'll die. Today, tomorrow maybe."

The monk nodded that he understood me and translated it to the others. Again nearly everyone spoke at once, and again the old guy raised his hands and silenced them. Then he spoke to the skinny one, who nodded and addressed me again.

"We have decided to make a ladder and try to get you out of the tree.

Please be patient."

Since I was pretty much out of options, I nodded my assent. I watched them for a while as they carefully picked the uprights, cut and stripped the bark, and went looking for the pieces that would become the steps. When they didn't return after a while I closed my eyes and drifted off to sleep. I dreamed an intense and fitful dream.

I was suddenly thirteen, and it was summer. My next-door neighbor was a pretty girl named Myrna. She was four days older than me, but I had a huge crush on her. We had whispered and plotted earlier in the day, and agreed to pretend to be asleep for the evening. She kissed my cheek, ran home, and was upstairs in no time. I mumbled something to my mom that I was sleepy, faked a big yawn, and raced upstairs too. I looked across at her window, but the curtains were drawn. I started to turn away when I saw her hand giving me the thumbs up sign, and then she pulled back the curtains and opened her window. She had shorts and a tee shirt on and was barefooted, and I watched her climb out the open window and beckon to me.

I jumped into my Levis and shirt and tugged on my window, but it was stuck. I panicked when she stepped to the tree and climbed down out of view. What was wrong with the stupid window? I braced and pushed up on the top frame, and heard a slight pop as the caulk along the glass broke loose. I stopped pushing and saw that the latch was still partly hooked. Within a moment I had joined her on the ground. She grabbed my hand and tugged me off towards the meadow.

We scampered down to the fence and ducked

under it into the meadow. Campfires and music and most of the people in the valley were already there. We tried to appear nonchalant and still be on the lookout for our parents, but there were so many people we never saw our folks. We had no trouble finding the huge wagon and team of horses that were tied to the hayride.

Within a moment we were in the wagon and over in a corner. I nodded to some older kids I knew. One girl scolded Myrna. "Your momma finds out you're here, and she'll tan your hide."

Myrna smiled sweetly and said, "If my momma finds out, we'll all know who told her, won't we." The older girl blushed and turned away as the wagon lurched into motion. The gentle bouncing of the wagon seemed to draw Myrna to me as if our bodies were magnets, and she was one charge and I was its opposite. Her leg was so close to me and her breasts were pushed against my shirt. I was almost afraid to breathe for fear of breaking the spell. So I just let the motion of the wagon rock me, with its gentle swaying. What a beautiful night, with the motion of the wagon rocking me...

For some reason something didn't seem right. It didn't quite smell like hay in the wagon, and I no longer felt Myrna against me. It smelled more like jungle.

Jungle? My eyes flew open! Dark night in a dark jungle greeted me. The swaying was not a hay wagon, but some sort of a stretcher. And I was tied into the stretcher, flat on my back. My hands were even tied to my side. I could only see the person just past my feet, gripping the rails of my stretcher. Was it a woman with a baldhead and a bare brown shoulder?

My heart sank as it dawned on me that I was back in the jungle. I was back in Viet Nam. And I was tied hand and foot, and being carried off in a direction I didn't know, and to a place I couldn't even imagine.

I had heard stories of the POW sites in Nam. They were mostly pits dug into the earth, with iron grates as doors. Most POWs didn't survive because they fed you nearly nothing, and dysentery stripped most of the guys of their will to live. My mood got as dark as the darkest part of the jungle night.

I was way too weak to think, and too tired to try to get up a plan of escape. And I was incredibly sore, with a fierce fire consuming my belly. I weighed my options and decided that being carried still had the advantage over walking, and I might just as well relax.

I was about to close my eyes when I realized that they had stripped me of my field uniform and put one of those orange robes on me.

I tried to process this information. Orange meant Buddhists. Buddhists were supposed to be pacifists, but most soldiers strongly suspected that the Buddhists were just a VC disguise. I remembered one grizzled Staff Sergeant from Special Forces telling me, "I just shoot 'em all. Let God sort **it** out." I remember him vividly because he also told me he had a Hmong wife, and that chewing beetle nuts was a great way to stay stoned and not lose your edge. His teeth were nearly black, and he drooled an almost constant stream of black juice down the side of his mouth.

I tried to move to get more comfortable, but couldn't. My uniform was gone, my belt was missing, and even the chain that held my dog-tags was gone!

"Hey, shit-heads!" I hollered. The articles of war,.. Geneva con..."

A firm hand clamped across my mouth. Above it a baldhead appeared. The old monk with the wispy goatee. He raised his other hand to his lips and whispered "Shhhh". The column came to a stop. I was pissed! I tried to speak through the hand that clamped on my mouth, but all that came out was a muffled something like "Gmmmmmmmmmm".

The old man shook his head no, holding his finger over his lips and trying to shush me. I looked into his eyes, which seemed surprisingly young on such a weathered old face. His eyes held a sadness that seemed to plead with me to be quiet. He took his left hand from his lips and pointed off to his left. Then his index finger pretended to point at my head. He dropped his thumb as if the hammer of the pistol had snapped. He may not know

English, but he was a great communicator. His hand went back to his lips for a final "Shhhh". I got real quiet.

In a couple of seconds that skinny young monk shuffled into view. He placed his hands together with his fingers pointing up and made a deep bow.

"Greetings," he whispered. "I am to tell you that we are all in great danger. We must be quiet. Soldiers are all around. If they see you are a foreigner they will shoot you for sure, and perhaps all of us too."

The old man finally took his hand off my mouth. "Where are you taking me?" I whispered hoarsely.

"We go to a temple." He answered, "You will be safe there as long as no one sees you." You must stay until you are strong enough to leave. Then the Abbot will decide about you."

"Are you Viet Cong?" I asked.

The young man smiled, "We are Buddhists. Buddhists do not participate in war. Buddhists practice harmlessness." He looked around conspiratorially. "Very difficult when you don't take sides. Both sides distrust you."

"What about me? I'm an American soldier?"

Putting his hand on the orange robe on my chest, he straightened it. "For now, you are a badly wounded monk who cannot talk. It's lucky for you that you are shorter than most Americans, and that you were born with brown eyes.

He winked and walked away before I could ask

him anything else. The column started again, and the gentle swaying went on and on. For a while I tried to figure out which direction we were going, but the night shadows told me nothing. My mind couldn't seem to get a handle on any plan, or any idea how to get out of the restraints. So I decided to relax and enjoy the fact that I was not walking.

A deep "gong" sound awakened me. I could feel myself reluctantly coming up and out of a dream I wasn't quite finished with. I tried to return to the dream, but now there was a sound of singing or something. When I finally opened my eyes I saw a flickering candle near the head of my bed. The fragrance of incense filled the room. As my eyes adjusted, I could see that old monk standing at the foot of my bed. He was saying or maybe singing something, and then the rest of the monks repeated him. This went on for a while, with each message repeated again and again, first the old guy, then the room

I lay there for a while, just taking it all in, and then I tried to sit up, but couldn't. I realized that I was still tied down.

"This is really getting old!" I croaked.

The room was suddenly silent. Only the whispered sound of the candle hissing and spluttering could be heard.

"Kind sir," a voice somewhere near my feet said, "You must not move too suddenly or you will burst the dressings on your wounds. It is only for this reason that you are restrained."

"Who are you?" I asked, blinking and trying to focus my eyes on the silhouette that now appeared beside the old monk.

Again the skinny one brought his hands together and bowed. "I am Troung."

He was all of five feet tall, and probably weighed less than 90 pounds.

"I want to be untied. I need to move and stretch."

He came to stand beside me and placed a hand on my forehead. I was hot and sweaty, and his hand seemed cool.

"You were severely wounded. Actually, you were impaled in a tree. Our physician has determined that you must be restrained. Also your ankle is swollen. If you try to walk and fall, you might bleed to death."

I let his words sort of roll around in my mind. "Shattered? Swollen? Bleed to death?" Not the kind of ·words I liked to hear when the talk is about me.

"Impaled in a tree?" I finally managed to say. Vague memories of wispy ghosts and long tunnels and...and...light. Was I remembering a dream, or what?

Troung removed a blanket and I could see my bloody and bandaged right foot. The old guy with the goatee and another even older one began unwrapping the blood soaked bandage.

The young monk smiled and bowed again, showing a five o'clock shadow on his shaved head. A flicker of a smile crossed his face. "We were afraid we would never be able to get you out of the tree. You were up nearly three meters, and you would strike out at us when we tried to help."

"What about the guys in my unit?" Another haunting memory fleetingly crossed my mind. I somehow knew they were all dead, but still I hoped I was wrong.

A shadow of sadness crossed the young monk's face. Just for a moment his eyes lowered. He drew in a long breath. Thirty-four souls departed their bodies. You and another one were the only ones who's spirits were intact."

"The other one, was he, uh, an American?"

The stubbly baldhead shook left to right. "She was a young Vietnamese.

She lost her foot. We may be able to save yours, though."

I knew that, although I didn't remember exactly why I knew it. Again I tried to clear my head. The memory of my First Sergeant instructor popped into my mind. He used to tell me over and over, "Get your head back in the game. Don't allow your mind to wander! Stay focused on what is real!"

My problem seemed to be a shifting perspective about what "real" was supposed to mean.

"You have been unconscious for many days." Troung said quietly. "We have had to restrain you each time we changed the dressing." He smiled. "It took all of the monks to hold you down. I shall return to shave your head. We must continue to present you as a fellow monk, in case we are visited by the soldiers.

Truong backed up and bowed and left. Now I was alone with the two older monks. They gently examined my right ankle, carefully unwrapping the soiled bandages.

After the dressing on my foot was changed, the two older ones removed the bandages from my belly and examined the angry red wound. They gently poked and prodded, and then rubbed some foul smelling potion on it. A new patch of old rag was taped across the wound and then they both bowed and left. I was alone. Alone but still tied up.

The guys in the squads used to sit around and talk about being captured. Basically there were two schools of thought. Some said you were better off being killed out-right, so start planning an escape attempt. The second idea was that staying alive was the main task. Keep a low profile and put all your energy into staying alive.

As I lay there in that damp bed, I tried to get a sense of my predicament. Either I had been rescued by the Buddhists and spared the horrors of letting the VC find me, or this was a temporary holding pattern, and they planned all along to turn me over to the enemy.

Technically I'm not a prisoner, although I am tied

up, and pretty well not able to move about freely. Maybe they are conning me, and I am a prisoner. But then, why the robe and the shaved head? Maybe they were just trying to save my life.

The more I thought about it, the more confused I became. Finally I decided not to decide anything, and just see what happens. With that handled, I had some serious sleeping to do.

The next days and weeks I had long bouts of unconsciousness, with wild and weird dreams in which I soared and sailed and rose and fell with the music of chanting voices and flickering candles.

Visions of my mother feeding me soup and spilling it on the orange robe were all mixed in with seeing the old goatee guy and Truong, and flying down the tunnel towards the light but not quite ever getting there. Once I heard my dad's voice calling me from the kitchen, "Get ready tonight, we're going duck hunting in the morning!" Then dad's face would melt into the face of the kindly old monk.

I would come awake when soup was poured into my mouth, and open my eyes to see if it was my mom or Truong. Later I would awaken with fever and chills and searing heat all around me. Sometimes, I woke myself up by peeing in my bed. At first I would worry that my dad would be furious at me, but the monks were so gracious, they just smiled and cleaned up the mess.

They would say things in Vietnamese, and I

came to understand they were saying, "It's okay, just lie back and don't worry." I remember thinking that if this is how they treated prisoners, then we must have had some really bad intel on them.

The rains came with a vengeance, and weeks and maybe months went by with rain all day and most of the night. There are two monsoon seasons in Viet Nam, the first begins in late March to early May. The other one comes around October. I had no clue which one this was. Once a week they came and shaved my face and head, and I took to gauging the passage of time with the shaves.

Truong was there every day, and he coached me on the language. Soon enough I had a rudimentary feel for the language. It amused me that the same words meant differing things by the tone in which they were said. But I caught on quickly.

One day he came in and started speaking English and I raised my hand and stopped him. "Speak only Vietnamese," I requested in Vietnamese. "I won't get better unless we use it."

He laughed and pointed out that he wouldn't get better in his English unless he used it, so we agreed every other day to use one or the other, but never both.

Some days it would rain so much that I could hear the roar of the rainfall all day and all night. I was getting better and trying to walk back and forth as a check on whether my belly was healing or not. At first it hurt so much that I would quit after three or four steps. My ankle seemed to hurt the more it rained, and it was raining almost continuously.

Then one day I woke up and knew that I had to strengthen my body to prepare for my departure. I got carefully get out of bed, and tried walking with my bad right foot. The first steps I nearly passed out with the pain, but as I came to anticipate it, I was able to manage better. I knew I had to get back the use of the foot if I ever planned on leaving.

The rain continued. Certain days it would roar on the corrugated tin roof so loudly that my ears hurt. I would get up and shuffle around, trying to put more weight on my right foot and ankle. I hobbled across the room to the door, and turned and headed back to the bed. When I turned again towards the door, I was startled to see the old Abbot standing there with Truong. I was surprised, but managed a deep bow and a formal greeting in Vietnamese. He smiled and took in the view of me walking and bowing.

"Perhaps," he said softly, "you would like to accompany Brother Truong the next time we discuss the Sutras." He bowed deeply and smiled and turned and left. Truong watched him go and raised his eyebrows to me.

"An invitation from the Abbot is nearly a command. Tell me you will join us. Today after the mid-day meal."

I nodded. Truong bowed and left me to my thoughts. I paced the floor all morning, ignoring the pain.

By the time Truong showed up, I was nearly worn out. I hobbled to the Great Room, where the main services are held. The old Abbot sat on a small pillow and bowed a greeting to us as we joined a circle of several monks.

I bowed to the other monks, and was shown a pillow at the far edge of the semi-circle that faced the old monk. For a while I just listened, trying to determine just how much of the language I understood. For the most part I was able to follow the discussions, and after Truong slipped me a pencil and a note pad, I scribbled down words and concepts that confused me. I found out that like Christianity, Buddhism has many denominations, or what they called schools.

This group was of the Zen tradition, and today's lecture was about the Bodhidharma's strong words. Strictly speaking, this teaching was outside the scriptures. We were urged to focus directly on the human heart. The Abbot spoke of continuous meditation outside the framework of sitting, in which a monk was to cultivate a choice-less and non-interfering awareness of simply noticing his thoughts. The key, as we were told, is to grasp at none of the thoughts. Notice and release. The simplicity of it reminded me of the state of mind a soldier carries into combat.

In combat the unfocused mind would allow for a peripheral vision and a noting of the activity, without ever directly allowing any subject to become the focus. This allowed the soldier to be open to everything, and respond without thinking.

The Abbot must have noticed the look on my face, because he asked me directly if I would like to comment. I stood and bowed, as is the protocol, and stammered that I was relating that kind of awareness to the mind of the soldier.

"Please give us an example," said the Abbot.

I spoke of the state of mind that came over me when I was in a combat situation. I had to keep asking Truong for words that I'd never learned, but the group waited with great patience until Truong and I found the word or concept, and then I would begin again in Vietnamese. Beloved Abbot, as the other monks referred to the old one, assured me that this was indeed the choice-less and non-interfering awareness that was referred to in the lecture. He mentioned that the Japanese had incorporated it into the Code of Bushido, or the warrior's code.

By the time the session was over, I was exhausted from the sheer effort of trying to explain complex ideas in a new language. When we finally stood and bowed and left the room, each of the other monks came to me and thanked me for being there. The old cook, with his scarred head and many scars, said, "You are welcome anytime to visit the kitchen and speak. I am an ex Viet Cong commander, and we share the way of the warrior."

He smiled knowingly, and bowed twice before he left. Truong walked with me back to my room and told me that he was sure the Abbot enjoyed my presence. "Would you join us again tomorrow?"

I wasn't sure that I didn't need a direct invitation from the Abbot, but Truong assured me that he would have been told if I weren't welcome.

And so I came to spend my days discussing philosophy or religion. One huge surprise came when I apologized for my faltering speech. The Abbot turned to me and quoted a passage from First Corinthians. He spoke in Vietnamese, but I easily recognized and translated these words: "And I, my brothers, when I came to you, did not come with excellence of speech, nor did I talk to you with learning of the mystery of God."

My jaw dropped, and I asked him where he had learned that quote. "Truth hides in every great book," he answered. "The trick is to find it and make it your own." The Sutras are revered commentaries on the teachings of the Buddha. I found plenty of similarities and plenty of differences between Buddhism and Christianity. Many a long discussion followed one of my questions. I got plenty of chances to perfect my

Vietnamese, and ask tons of questions. The Abbot patiently answered and explained in detail the philosophy of Buddhism. But he seemed to be just as familiar with the other religions as he was with his Buddhism.

As the days passed and the season changed yet again, my foot resisted a total healing. It pained me to walk any distance, and I still became tired after a short time of any type of exercise. I knew that I needed to be going, but worried that I was too weak to survive any sort of a trek.

I tried without success to interrogate Truong about the location of the monastery. He claimed he didn't even know which province it was in. Although I liked him and enjoyed talking and kidding with him, I wasn't sure I could trust him. So I told no one that I was planning on leaving.

One day Truong and I were discussing meditation. This time we were talking about the formal sitting meditation. "What do you think about when you sit for all those hours? Is it like praying?"

Truong didn't answer right away. I thought maybe he hadn't heard me, or was just avoiding an answer. He did this often enough that I had decided to just wait him out. I just stared at him and waited, and waited. I was about to explain to him that ignoring a question in my culture would be considered rude. He smiled and spoke slowly. "Meditation is a way to turn the mind inward, away from the world. We meditate before we decide almost every action. We seek to understand the rightness of our actions. Do you remember the talk of Beloved Abbot's about right-mindedness giving rise to right action?"

I nodded. The memory of the discussion with a bundle of light still bothered me, but I had no intention of telling Truong, or anyone else about that.

"Do you ask hard questions?" I asked.

Truong furrowed his brow. The wrinkles stopped just short of the place on his head where a hairline would be if he had any hair. "Hard questions?"

"You know, like should I eat meat? Should I go back to being a soldier?

Should I shave my head today? Hard, specific questions!"

"Beloved Abbot tells us that when we are not sure of anything that we should ask within. If we get a sense of direction, then we would do well to follow it. When we get no clear answer then we know that it is an indication that we should simply wait. The answer will come."

He studied me for a moment and announced. "Tomorrow I shall bring a razor, and both of us can shave. You are beginning to not look like a Buddhist."

With that he bowed ever so slightly and left.

"Well, I'll meditate on that," I said, loud enough

for him to hear through the closed door.

"No sense of humor," I muttered to the empty room. I was definitely getting stir-crazy. The continuous rain, the passage of day after day, the way my foot refused to get better.

"Another day and I'll go insane," I said aloud. I flopped onto the end of the cot and, just for the hell of it straightened my spine like I had seen the monks do.

I drew in a deep breath, held it, and slowly exhaled. I had seen this routine so often it was nothing to duplicate it. I allowed my eyes to close, and listened and focused on breathing in, hold, breathe out, in, hold, out. I decided if I was going to pretend to be a Buddhist, then I might as well look the part. Besides, there isn't much else to do. I'll gain their trust if I look like I'm getting on with the program.

There doesn't seem to be a lot to this, I thought. As my breathing became slow and regular I thought about my escape. It wasn't about whether I should leave or not, it was more about when. An idea popped into my head. One minute I was following my breath, and the next I got this notion. It told me to prepare, and leave the first day the rain stopped.

I opened my eyes, and glanced around. That idea was so clear, and so sure. I immediately wondered if that might mean the Viet Cong came out of hiding and started patrols again. Funny, I thought. The war gets put on hold when the weather is bad.

I argued with the idea for most of the day, and into the night. But in the morning it was still there. Still clear, and still unambiguous, it spoke with authority. "Leave when the rain stops," it said.

Maybe that was what Truong was talking about, the idea that a clear answer is clear. And I certainly couldn't pretend that it was fuzzy.

I went to the lectures with Beloved Abbot, but my mind was busy planning. I had to make up a list of essentials I would need for my escape. I decided I had to start hoarding food and storing it under the bed. I would need a canteen, and a good pair of boots, or at least good sandals. The locals were very thrifty, and all over Viet Nam you could find sandals made out of heavy canvass uppers and cut up tires for soles. I asked Truong if he could get me a pair of sandals, and the next day they were lying at the foot of my bed.

Later I told Truong how much I enjoyed the discussions, but that I needed to walk longer distances.

"This is good," he said, "but you must never go out alone. We have signals that tell us when the soldiers are coming, but we still can't take the chance that you would be seen."

"How long have I been here?" I asked.

Truong thought for a moment and said, "Nearly four months. Why?"

"*Four months!*" My mind recalled the announcements of the Secretary of State, and the promised withdrawal of troops. Good morning Viet Nam broadcasts just before the rescue attempt had indicated that troop strength was down to 12,000. If I had been there four months, then I might be one of the last Americans in the country. I had to get a plan going and get out of here! My foot still pained me but my belly was mostly healed.

Truong must have been reading my mind. He smiled and looked out the window. "I have so much enjoyed our discussions with the Abbot. You ask such good questions.

Chapter 4

I decided to start and end each day with a meditation. Part of me said it was done to impress the monks that I was becoming Buddhist. Another part of me thought it was a good idea all on its own. It seemed to ease the restlessness in me, and also offer me more ideas and options.

At the very next session with the Abbot, he spent the entire time stressing the importance of meditation on a daily and regular basis.

"One must never confuse formal meditation with the continuous process of observing the mind from a detached place." He looked at me and smiled and continued. "It often helps to imagine yourself floating upwards from the body.

This allows a sense of being more than the body, and simply an observer of the actions of the world."

The hair on the back of my head would have been standing at attention if there had been any. The thought occurred to me that this little man could actually read my mind. He winked at me. A feeling of panic engulfed me and he smiled again.

His eyes wandered around the room, pausing on each monk before returning to meet my gaze. "It may even help," he continued, "to see this part of yourself as form of light."

I decided that I had better start practicing the poker face that I used to use so well back at the camp. He nodded ever so slightly and continued to explain formal meditation. I wondered if he would be willing to teach me to read minds, but he never looked again in my direction.

That evening I sat on the edge of my bed and closed my eyes. I tried to listen to my breathing, but my mind was jumping around from idea to idea. I felt like there was no privacy when an old man might be hearing my thoughts as I thought them. Did that mean he knew that I was planning on leaving?

I shook my head, trying to clear my mind of these troubling thoughts, and suddenly got the strong urge to sit on the floor, cross-legged, like the other monks did.

At first it was awkward, but by sitting on my pillow I elevated my butt enough to be able to get my legs crossed with each foot above the other knee. I smiled to myself and thought that the monks would be proud of me.

I remembered to not "attach" my mind to that thought, or any other and idly noticed the pattern of my breath. Shortly my thoughts slowed to where there seemed to be an interval between each idea. I remembered thinking that this might be exactly what the Abbot was talking about, and then smiled as I remembered his closing words. He had bowed to each of us and repeated to each of us, "Avoid spiritual pride."

I stayed sitting and breathing for a long time. I wasn't sure if this was meditating or not, but took pride in the fact that I at least looked the part.

Following the Abbot's instructions I said silently "Inward," each time I drew in a breath. "Hold" was for the resting time, and "Outward" with each time I let the breath go. My mind got real quiet after a while, almost like no thoughts at all.

Suddenly I was back at the ambush, throwing my left arm around that boy in the black pajamas. I thought I heard the sound of the black knife as it entered his ribcage. I tensed as the boy collapsed into my arms.

I seemed to rise up out of my body just as the wispy form of the boy appeared above his corpse. Both of us glanced back on the spectacle of blood and jungle. Then the wispy form of the boy smiled at me and took my hand, pulling me into the air.

"Get the hell away from me!" I screamed. My eyes flew open and I tried to stand, but my legs were asleep. I stepped with my bad foot, and collapsed in a heap on the earthen floor. I muffled another scream, worried that the monks might come to check on me.

I crawled over to the bed and managed to pull myself up enough to collapse onto the cot. Sweat ran down my face, stinging my eyes and soaking my orange robe. My legs hurt from sitting, and my mind was churning.

The intensity of the meditation and the strange vision of that boy tumbled around in my mind. Was there some meaning I was supposed to get? What the hell was happening to me? I needed to straighten out my mind, and I needed to get a grip on reality.

Maybe I was being brain-washed with some drugs they were putting into my meals. I started to get up and pace, but the pain from my foot and ankle made that impossible. I lay back down on the cot, but never slept at all. Just before dawn, I heard the gong for morning sitting, and decided I was through with that crap. With that decision made, I finally fell asleep.

Truong must have checked on me, since we usually walked together to the morning meditation. But if he did, he must have decided to let me be. I slept through the mid-day meal like I was dead.

I woke up to the sound of pouring rain on the tin roof, soaked in my own sweat and stinking so much I disrobed and stood naked in the rain outside my door. I used the last of the coarse soap to try to scrub the memories of the night from me, but returned to my cot feeling confused, angry and frustrated.

Late in the day Truong tapped on the door and entered. "Are you feeling all right," he asked in Vietnamese. "The Abbot has asked about you."

I lay flat on my back with my eyes closed. "Tell him no! Never again! And you stay away from me too!" He nodded and left.

I thought about the idea of sitting in that temple, with the Abbot reading my mind, and a sense of sheer terror filled me. I was convinced that I had been brain-washed, and suspected that maybe hypnosis was being used. The last thing I wanted to do was give them more opportunities to get inside my head. I had to get away from this place, back with my unit, if it was still in

The Viet Cong was the enemy! I am an American soldier. These things were the basics. Maybe the Buddhists had rescued me, and tried to treat me medically, but they could not be trusted.

I undid my robe and examined my belly. It was still purple and red and sore as hell. I guess I'm lucky no vital organs were damaged. I wondered how that tree branch managed to get all the way through me without puncturing my intestines. A noise at the door jerked me back to the moment. I covered myself and opened the door, expecting to see someone standing there.

A bowl of rice soup and some veggies wrapped in a leaf had been placed at my doorstep. I panicked, thinking that they were still trying to slip me some drugs that would make it easier to hypnotize me. I glanced towards the temple, hoping to catch sight of the cook, but there wasn't a sign of anyone. I shut the door with the food outside.

I remembered the old cook. He had whispered that he used to be a commander in the Viet Cong. Maybe he still was.

I sat again on the cot, trying to sort things out. I couldn't very go without food if I hoped to gain my strength. And if I stayed in my room, then they couldn't hypnotize me. Or could they?

It got good and dark before I moved again. My mind seemed unable to focus. Nothing made any sense anymore. I had to get out of here, and I had to get better to make it happen. And I was afraid to ask for anything from anyone. I couldn't even talk to Truong anymore, for fear that he was somehow a part of the plan to... to what? I flung myself back on the bed and stared at the ceiling.

It was either my stomach growling, or some other noise that woke me. It was pitch dark, and raining. I opened the door and found the food, which had mostly managed to avoid the downpour.

I slurped the cold soup and ate the vegetables without thinking. I had to maintain my strength. I placed the bowl outside my door and returned to bed, and slept hard.

Morning prayer gong brought me out of my deep sleep. I opened my eyes and stared at the ceiling. No good ideas magically appeared. No bad ones either. In fact my mind seemed too numb to even form a coherent thought. A gentle rapping at the door brought me out of my stupor.

Truong opened the door but didn't enter. "Are you feeling better? I see that you ate. Are you going to morning prayer?"

"No," I said, surprised at the croaky sound of my own voice. "But please come in."

He glanced at the downpour and entered closing the door.

"How big was the branch?" I asked. He looked at me like he had no idea what I was talking about.

"You know, I was up in the tree, with a branch sticking out of me. How big was the branch?"

Truong frowned and his eyes went to my belly. He made a circle using his thumb and index finger, about the size of a Ping-Pong ball.

I wondered if he was teasing me. "That would have killed me," I said. "I'd be dead for sure!"

I asked him again, and again he gave the same

response. "Shouldn't I be dead?"

A slow smile spread across his face. "Maybe yes, maybe no. Here you are though. Are you coming to morning sitting?"

I shook my head and closed my eyes. He was gone when I reopened them.

He checked on me the next day and again I asked him in. "Do you ever get the idea that Beloved Abbot can read your mind?"

A big grin appeared. "Of course he can. He teaches us that if we quiet our mind, we can hear the trees, the moon, and the thoughts around us." He opened his mouth to say more, but then decided against it.

"What? What were you going to say, and didn't?"

He rolled his eyes. "You were angry and didn't attend the day he lectured about that. I was going to remind you of what he said, and then remembered that you were not present."

"I'm not sure what I think or believe anymore." I muttered.

Truong just stood there.

"I can buy some of this stuff," I told him. "Like the First Noble Truth; All life is suffering. But I'm not so sure I can go along with Number Two. Can suffering be alleviated?"

He drew in a long breath and just stood there for the longest time with his eyes half closed. It was as if he had to go and check his memory before he spoke. I had heard the Abbot when he spoke of what he called the contemplative life. The theory was that some part of our mind knows. The tendency to speak without accessing this part of the mind is a cause of much suffering, and so before we speak we ask within. It was all supposed to be part of the eight-fold path. "Right thinking leads to right speaking, right speaking leads to..."

I could almost see the little old Abbot as he conducted his lecture, but for the life of me I couldn't remember what followed right thinking. So I guessed that Truong was checking his memory before he answered. He did that a lot.

His habit of waiting to answer was always annoying, but today it seemed downright rude. I was just about to tell him so again when he nodded and spoke.

"In order to give up suffering, we must be first willing to give up our attachments. Beloved teacher spoke many times about this, and I know you were present."

I smiled sarcastically. "So it's not the rain, but my attachment to wanting it to stop?"

"Ah," Truong responded. "That is such an excellent example! Yes. Rain is just rain. What we think of the rain causes us to suffer. Not the rain, but the thought. Exactly!"

I thought about the people of Viet Nam. Their history was filled with war, with conquering foreigners. They had so little to say about the armies that roared back and forth, destroying and killing as they went, Chinese, French, Japanese, and now us Americans. No wonder they concluded that it was their thoughts that caused them pain. At least there was a small hope of controlling their thoughts.

Truong smiled and spoke. "Beloved Abbot teaches us that it is not even physical sensations that hurt us. It is the pain of resistance to the sensations. We want things to be different, and our anger at them not being different brings suffering."

Immediately my mind raced to the conclusion that maybe he too could read my mind. I glared at him but refused to allow another question to form in my mind.

We sat in silence for a while. I didn't dare say all the things I suspected, and he seemed to want to wait me out.

Finally he said, "Aren't you coming to hear the Abbot anymore?"

I shook my head. He nodded and stood and bowed," Beloved Abbot always tells us that if we take care about the moment, that the future will take care of itself."

"Do you believe him?" I asked

"The Abbot's life is his proof." Truong said softly. "We learn mindfulness is all that is required of us. This means we commit only to noticing our thoughts. We release any angry ones, and dedicate our mind to being the silent observer."

"Do you hate me?" I asked. His face showed surprise. I was thinking of the boy on the last patrol.

"How could I hate you?" he answered.

I thought about the many patrols, the ambushed, and the kills. A small black bug crawled past my good foot as I sat on the edge of the bed. I squashed it without thinking.

Truong's face started to register surprise, and he then went quickly to a passive mask.

"I try to remember that harmlessness is a way of life," he said. "But I too, forget sometimes. If there are ever soldiers present, your very life may depend upon your remembering." He turned toward the door, but then turned back to me.

"And I must remember that my duty is to observe my own mind and not stand in judgment of another. Beloved Abbot reminds us that condemnation is nothing more than a sly form of attack. And attack is never practicing harmlessness." And with that comment he turned and left.

The days slid by in a haze of dreariness. The dampness got inside me, chilling me to the bone and even chilling my mind. I slept in bursts and starts, awake for most of the nights and some of the days. I stopped allowing my head to be shaved, and my beard came in ragged and wild.

Truong never came back after I refused to let him shave me, and the only marks of time were the gongs that called them to meditate and dine. My food was delivered silently twice each day. Each day I ate half of the food, carefully saving anything that I might be able to take with me. I placed it against the wall at the back corner of the top of my bed.

One morning my own guttural scream woke me from a fitful night of sleep. I sat on the edge of the bed and tried to shake the sleep from my mind. I straightened my spine and began the process of deep breathing.

I needed to rid my mind of the terrifying images of enemy soldiers and explosions and screams, the silent sounds of my own weapon chattering in slow motion as the shells impacted the bodies. I consciously tried to remember the faces of my mom and dad, but nothing came. I panicked at the thought that I was so far removed from everything I loved that I couldn't even get a clear picture of my parents' faces.

No sooner would a vague picture of my parents appear than it would be replaced by a face of an enemy soldier. Each face would silently scream at me to stop, whether it seemed to be Mom or Dad or the enemy, the message was always the same.

If I had been back at the unit, I would have requested a chaplain. The guys called it wigging out, and now I knew what they were talking about. I was definitely wigging out.

But there was no chaplain. And I was not back in my unit. And that damned rain was never going to quit.

Once I allowed my mind to move upwards and away from the images. I drifted up to a place where I could imagine that I could see myself sitting on the edge of the cot. I imagined seeing the top of my own head, and noticing the posture of a man at the ragged edge of crisis. I wanted to reach out and comfort that form of myself. I imagined I actually did reach out and place a hand on my own forehead, and immediately felt a sense of peace calm me.

I was so startled by the sudden change, the sudden sense of peace that I came quickly out of the meditation.

"Huh, I snorted. What just happened?

I stood and stretched and noticed for the first time that the day was very bright. And there was no sound of rain. I listened carefully. Nothing. The silence almost hurt.

I quickly washed, noticing the stiff and bristly beard, and the hair that once again covered my head. Today, I decided, I would shave again. I need to look like a Buddhist to succeed in the escape.

I sighed and hobbled outside and headed towards the well. I drew a bucket and ladled some of it into my bowl. Buddhists drink from the same vessel that they eat from, and I decided to get used to their routines. The sun was bright and hot as I moved backwards against the building, stepping out of the sunlight and into the cooling shadows of a large tree.

A movement in the corner of my eye caught my attention. It was a small figure, even smaller that Truong. The head was shaved, and whoever it was moved slowly with the aid of two homemade crutches. Was it a girl? I squinted in the bright morning light.

Whoever she was, she seemed so intent on getting to the garden that she never even glanced in my direction. She was obviously new to the crutches, and very awkward in her movements. She cried out or winced with nearly every movement, and my first reaction was to go and help.

Buddhists discourage any contact between genders, and so I decided to wait and watch her progress. I didn't even know there were any nuns in the temple, and certainly no wounded ones. Maybe she was an acolyte, like myself.

I waited while she made her way past me and into the courtyard. My eyes were drawn to her foot. Not feet, but foot. She had only one foot.

I had a bowl full of water in my hand, and started to raise it to drink, but realized I was no longer thirsty. My heart went out to her. I blessed her for her courage to try to get around on just one foot. She had a lot of courage that one. She hobbled over to my favorite place and sat down.

I noticed that I had become sort of territorial about the garden. I had so often braved the rain and sat under the overhanging roof of the temple, it was a place to go and think and not be bothered. I watched my mind struggle with empathy for her and anger that she had taken my favorite place in the garden.

For a moment I considered returning to my room, but then I decided that this garden was as much mine as it was hers to use. And I really needed to do some thinking.

I sighed and stepped out of the shadow of the tree and moved towards the garden. I was moving slowly, and yet still my foot miscalculated a small step causing me to lurch. She jerked her head at the sound of my approach, and clamored to her feet, grabbing a crutch. "Stay away!" she hissed.

I stopped in my tracks. I studied her for a moment and extended the bowl. "Water?" I muttered. I was close enough that she could have taken it.

Her face was a mask of hatred. Her eyes darted up and down, taking me in. For some reason I wished I had a fresh shave. I extended the bowl closer, spilling some of the water at her feet.

She lashed out with the crutch and knocked the bowl to the floor, spilling most of the water onto her robe. The bowl bounced once and landed on its rim and spun like a tired top. Both of us watched in silence as it spun round and around and around again on its rim, making a noise that got louder and louder as it went. It finally stopped. The silence suddenly seemed too loud.

I muttered in Vietnamese, "I just thought you might like some water."

She turned her back to me, so I hobbled past her to a place out of the sun and sat on a stone bench. I deliberately turned away from her, and studied the contents of the pond. I had been so long with the monks I thought I knew everyone at the monastery. Who was she, and why was she here?

Maybe she was a recent rescue. Whoever she was, she definitely was not friendly. I wondered if she would contact the closest authority and have me arrested. She must have noticed I was a foreigner. Whatever peace of mind I had hoped to find in the garden had vanished, and my mind was jumbled with this new discovery.

The murmur of the brook sounded suddenly threatening, the white flowers in the pond seemed like ghosts. The garden that used to calm me and afford such peace now seemed like an ambush about to happen.

I looked around, my senses on full alert, with memories of patrols and firefights filling my mind. My breathing was shallow and rapid. For the first time in months I could actually taste the bitter fear in my dry mouth. The thump, thump of my heart and the shallowness of breath told me that I was no longer in a safe place.

My months of recovery and long discussions of

philosophy had suddenly ended. I had an almost uncontrollable urge to cry.

I decided to try the methods I had learned to still my racing mind, but had no luck at all. I wanted to outwait her so that I wouldn't have to pass her again when I left, so I just sat there. Once or twice I opened one eye and checked the movement of the shadows.

She had to be Viet Cong! How else could I explain the wounds, and the hatred at seeing me? And if she were Viet Cong, she'd do everything in her power to tell them of my presence and have me arrested. Suddenly I hated the temple and needed to be gone.

I waited with my eyes closed as long as I could and then glanced in her direction. She was gone. I stood stiffly and shuffled back towards my room. I needed to find Truong and get some straight answers.

The door that I had always assumed was a storage room stood ajar, and a heap of orange rags was keeping it from closing. Two crutches had been propped beside the door. I went to move the rags and saw a pool of blood and a small hand.

"Truong!" I yelled. "Please help! Anyone!" I kneeled down and lifted her into my arms and kicked the door open.

An old nun appeared and stared at me. "Give her to me!" she commanded. The nun was tiny, maybe four and a half feet tall. On a good day she might have weighed 75 pounds. I could just imagine me handing the girl to her and watching her drop her.

"Get out of my way," I said. "And hold the door open!"

She swallowed and bowed and pushed the door wider. I went in and gently placed the girl on the bed. "She needs help," I said. The old nun nodded and pointed at the door. No words were needed to tell me that I wasn't needed or allowed in this room.

Inside was a cot like mine, and a nightstand. "This girl has fallen. She needs help," I said again.

The nun's face contorted into a mask of rage. "Get away from her! Leave! Now! Again she pointed a bony finger at the door.

I hobbled back to my room and flopped onto the bed. My mind was jumbled and bruised. Too many images! Too many disconnected thoughts for one day. I could still feel the softness of the girl's body against my chest. I could still taste the fear in my mouth.

What did all this mean? It meant I had to get the hell out of here, that's what it meant! I closed my eyes and held them tightly shut for a long time. Mercifully, I must have drifted off to sleep.

The sweat had gathered in my eye sockets. A stinging sensation pulled me out of sleep, and I awakened to find myself lying on my back in a pool of sweat, inside a very hot room that seemed to have no air at all. I groaned and sat up. My clothes were soaked. My foot hurt. My belly hurt. But most of all my brain hurt. Funny how one day could change things. I had to leave and soon. I gave up on the idea of staying until I felt healed.

I wanted it to have been so different. I wanted to be healed in the belly, and healed in the foot and ankle. I wanted to be back with my unit. I wanted to believe I could even find my unit, or any other unit of American troops.

And then the thought of the girl came creeping back into my mind. I remembered holding her unconscious body in my arms. I wanted to just hold her and protect her. I wanted her to listen as I told her how sorry I was for her pain, and for her wounds.

I wanted to tell her that I knew who she was. I wanted to tell her it was my weapon that took her foot, and tore through her body and nearly took her life. And I knew she hated me, and couldn't wait to signal some VC unit, and have me taken out and shot. And I knew I had to get the hell out of here!

I lurched to my feet and hobbled outside, hoping for cooler air. I almost tripped on the bowl of food, and cursed under my breath when I put my bad foot down too fast to keep me from falling.

I was starved! And so I knelt down and took the bowl and the wrapped vegetables, and the tiny pot of tea, and headed for the garden. Mercifully, I was its only occupant. I remembered to slow down my mind and savor each slurp of tea. I ate half of each vegetable roll, and half of the sticky rice. I would stash the saved food under my bed with all the rest.

I sat for a while and watched the day turn into night. Finally, I picked up the bowl and teapot and made my way back to my room. I left the door open, hoping to get some breeze to cool it down. I placed the bowl and pot at the door, slid the saved food under the bed and laid down. I was almost immediately asleep.

"Brother Toby?" came Truong's soft voice.

I sat up in the pitch darkness. "I came with your mid-day meal, but you were nowhere in sight."

"And where were you when I needed to ask you some questions? Who is that girl?" My voice was louder than it needed to be and I consciously toned it down. "Is she Viet Cong? Is she the other survivor of my last mission?"

Truong let himself in and smiled. "Yes and yes. There is much commotion since you picked her up and entered her room, too."

"What was I supposed to do, let her die in the doorway? Is that the Buddhist way? Don't touch a member of the opposite sex, just let them die?"

He took his time answering, but then that was nothing new. Sometimes I think he only did that to try to look wise, or to piss me off.

"Surely you must remember that you two came to the temple together. There were only two survivors."

I knew who she was. I had just hoped I was wrong. I guess I had hoped that the one I shot had died, and this one was somehow a different one. But I also knew that was just bullshit. The memory of that young girl lying next to her foot wouldn't leave my mind.

He studied me for what seemed like five minutes. I was determined to outwait him.

Finally he frowned and drew a deep breath. Each word came out slowly, as if he was having trouble with the translation. "There was a heated discussion when we found the two of you. Most of the monks said it would bring only trouble to our temple to bring you two back here." He smiled sadly, "I had almost convinced myself they were wrong until today. Guests in a monastery are never supposed to have any contact with a person of the opposite gender."

"We ran into each other in the garden. I had no idea she was here, or even alive," I muttered darkly.

He nodded. "I see," he said softly. I could tell he didn't see at all. "The Lord Buddha admonishes us to have right-minded thinking and right- minded actions." He frowned again, "You did not speak to her, did you?"

"I never heard it was against the law to speak

to a... female!" He nodded his head up and down.

"Hey!" I said. "I never took any vows! I agreed to listen to what you guys had to say, but only to pass the time until I got better." It occurred to me that I may have said more than I wanted to.

He held up his hand. "Promise me you will not speak to her again. Please try to stay away from her. If you see her..."

"If I see her I'll damned well hide!" I retorted. "She made it clear that she hates me and will have me killed if she gets the chance."

His voice was as soft as mine was loud. "Then you will honor us by keeping our customs?"

A part of me was mad at him for suspecting me of making a pass at her. I didn't think I had. Another part of me was mad at myself for remembering with such intensity the feelings and sensations of softness that I had when I held her in my arms.

"So I should not have helped her when she collapsed?" I asked quietly.

Truong tilted his head and was still for some time. "It is wrong for you to offer her water in the garden. It is wrong to speak to her. But one never turns away from someone in distress."

" I am sorry for my poor manners," I said. I bowed to him formally. "Please forgive my lack of knowledge of your customs. I don't fully know all of your ways."

He was still for some time, and then

returned the bow. "Forgive me, Brother Toby. I have spoken so harshly. I must admit that sometimes I wish I could look upon her and speak to her. Sometimes I am weak in my commitment to the Path of Buddha."

I smiled and slapped him on the arm. "Hey! We are men, remember? We all have our moments of weakness."

He didn't smile back, and he didn't get my attempt at teasing. He bowed again and started to leave. I held up my hand and he paused.

"What should I do if I see her again?" I asked.

"You won't," he said softly. She has re-injured herself, and may not live long."

"How can I know if she contacted the enemy?"

He shook his head. "Today was the first time she was able to stand or leave her room. She is now unconscious, and someone is with her all the time."

He stepped through the open door, and turned back to me. "And besides," he said, "If she contacts the "enemy" all of us would probably be shot. Not just you."

I lay down on my bed and tried to sleep. I kept reliving that moment of raking my weapon across that column of soldiers, and seeing in slow motion the impact of each shell on the bodies of the men and the girl. I remembered letting up on the trigger after she lost her foot, and I remembered the last two impacts; one in her mid-section and one in the shoulder.

I tried to will it so that I stopped firing before she was hit, but that picture refused to form in my mind. There is something thankfully impersonal about killing the enemy. You don't know them. You don't relate to them at any level. They become targets. Nothing more. Now all that was changed.

Killing had seemed so normal. So necessary! And yet the amputation of a limb seemed so barbaric, so, so inexcusable. Was it just because I had met her? I had offered her water. I had actually held her in my arms. Felt her vulnerability?

Damn this war! And damn those memories I can't seem to lose! I lay there for a long time, but couldn't fall asleep.

Finally I sat up and decided to go again to the garden. I softly stepped outside and was very careful to step carefully so as not to slip or make a misstep. It was very dark, with no moon to help me. I had to feel my way along the path, past the fountain and to my favorite place. I started to ease onto the bench. A sudden shove nearly made me jump out of my skin.

"Go away!" a voice hissed.

I caught myself and tried to focus my eyes into the dark shadows. "What are you doing here?" I finally managed to say.

As my eyes adjusted to the darkness, I saw her staring at my sore foot. "At least you still have your foot. You shot mine off!"

I rubbed my eyes and drew a deep breath. "I was told you were unconscious...near death. I am glad to see you are not."

She laughed an angry hollow laugh. "I waited until the old lady fell asleep. I intend to go and find some comrades."

I took a deep breath, searching for the right words, "If there was any way I could undo that day, and that firefight, I would. I... I am so sorry, so really sorry that you lost your foot."

Her eyes bore into mine. "I didn't lose it! You shot it off! And I would kill you now if I had a way!"

I bowed my head. "I have to go. We are not supposed to ever talk to each other."

"The next time I see you, I will kill you." I nodded.

She looked at me with all the hatred she could muster. I turned and shuffled back to my room.

I knelt and searched under the bed for the pieces of fruit I had stashed. My hand hit something large and unexpected. I placed my face right down on the earthen floor and reached as far back under the bed as I could. Every time I felt something I took it out and examined it. It felt like Christmas.

The first thing I pulled out was an army issue canteen, still in the canvass carrier, and filled with fresh water. Then I found my beloved black K-bar knife. I tested the blade and found it incredibly sharp. Next came my pocket Bible.

As I held the Bible in my hand I felt something sharp and irregular imbedded in the front cover. I stood up and examined it. A huge piece of shrapnel was stuck through the first half of the book. I opened it and found the first page that wasn't mangled was the Book of Psalms. I tossed it aside and dived back to see what else I could find.

My arm stretched back and landed on a bundle of cloth, tied with a coarse brown string. I pulled it out and discovered it was my cammie uniform, both the pants and the shirt. They had been washed and folded. Next to them was an empty backpack.

There were several large fruits called Maniocs. Each one would make a full meal. There were lots of egg rolls wrapped in wax paper, and last but not least the small bits of food I had stashed.

I sat on the edge of the bed and opened the Bible. Psalm 11: "In the Lord I put my trust: how say ye to my soul, Flee as a bird to your mountain."

That must mean that I'm supposed to escape from these Buddhists, right?

But maybe this is the mountain I was supposed to flee to. This was not making much sense.

I read on: "The Lord trieth the righteous; but the wicked and him that love violence his soul hateth."

These heathen Buddhists said that they practiced non-violence. What did the Lord think of all the men I had killed? Would the Lord love these

Buddhists and hate me because I killed in a war? The Old Testament was filled with war, slaying ten thousand here and a thousand there. Is war good or bad?

I lay in bed and smiled. I had thought I was being so sneaky about leaving, and every monk must have known all along. And instead of trying to stop me, they gave me the things they thought I needed.

Just then I was sure I heard a noise right outside my door. I sprang up and pulled the door wide. The old cook stood there with a machete. I jumped back and eyed my K-bar on the bed. He could kill me before I got to it.

My first thought was that the girl had sent him to kill me, but he smiled and bowed and handed the machete to me, handle first.

With his bare hand he made the motion of slashing, and pointed to the jungle. In Vietnamese he said, "This will help. You need a sharp one, right?"

I fingered the blade and smiled. Bowing deeply I thanked him. He backed out of the door and pulled it silently shut. Through the closed door I heard him call, "Go in peace!"

I was ready to go at first light. I lay down and slept deeply for the first time in many days.

Chapter 5

I slept fitfully and woke up way before the prayer gong. The sun was still at least an hour from rising as I ate some sticky rice and a chunk of manioc. It took only a few minutes to pack my newly acquired items. I stayed in the room until I heard Truong's gentle tap. "I won't be going to morning prayers," I called through the closed door.

I listened as Truong padded away and the other monks shuffled by my door towards the temple. I allowed an extra five minutes to avoid the chance of encountering any stragglers. I could only hope that the VC girl wasn't up and about.

I straightened the bedcover and put the room in order and made one last check under the bed to make sure I was leaving nothing. Way back in one corner I found another canvass covered canteen filled with water. A silent prayer of thanks went out to the kind soul who provided it. Sometimes all that separated life from death was one canteen of drinkable water. I packed the backpack tightly and opened the door.

The pre-dawn chill was in the air, but my spirits were high. I knew I needed to be on the move, and just the very thought of a journey pleased me. I made my way as quietly as I could to the side gate in the garden, first making sure that girl was not lurking in some shadow.

The monks had a water feature and pond, so I followed the path of the water and quickly found a small stream. Although I wore the robes of the monk, I looked obviously different toting two canteens and a full backpack. Besides, not many monks carried a machete.

The sandals from Truong were fine for walking, but offered no protection for my bandaged foot. And since I was reluctant to follow the stream for fear of encountering an enemy patrol, I tried out my new machete and hacked my own trail, staying always near the gentle gurgle of the stream.

I knew that if I followed a small stream it would lead to a bigger one, maybe even to a larger river.

After nearly three hours of hacking and sweating I paused to wipe the sweat from my brow. I decided to give it another twenty hacks with the machete before a break for lunch. On hack number fourteen I nearly fell into a river. It was swollen with the long monsoon rains and had risen to a flood stage. There was virtually no bank at all. If I had been leaning the wrong way I would have plunged right into it.

I stopped and gazed in amazement. Its muddy green water flowed rapidly towards the rising sun, which meant I could possibly ride it all the way to the sea.

I sighed deeply, noticing for the first time how concerned I had been about the location of the monastery. I knew that the rivers and streams in the central highland near the DMZ either flowed west to the upper Mekong River, or east to the South China Sea. And since I had no desire to head into Laos, my chances of locating either The ARVN or allied forces seemed much more promising if I could travel towards the sea.

After a quick lunch and a drink from the canteen, I hacked some large branches off a couple of trees. With an eye towards keeping myself from being seen, I managed to create a crude raft that could not only float me in relative comfort but hide me from prying eyes. Fashioning the raft took up all of the rest of the daylight and into the evening. As the last rays of sunlight filtered through the heavy canopy of trees I surveyed my work. I sure hoped it would look like just another pile of drifting tree limbs to the casual observer.

My belly was hurting from swinging the machete, and my foot had started to seep blood. I took care to unwrap the bandage and wash it in the cleaner part of the river. Then I rewrapped it and made a tiny fire to heat tea water. It took forever to come to a boil, and I let it hiss for a while, hoping to burn out most of the impurities from the muddy water. I dared not waste any of the precious water from the canteens. After pouring a small amount into the bowl and adding some tea, I emptied the rest into the half-filled canteen, taking care not to pour so fast that it would spill.

Finally I allowed myself to enjoy the tea, savoring every sip. A wave of exhaustion swept over me and I stretched out on the ground. My belly hurt, and my foot throbbed and seeped a little blood. Knowing I had to eat to maintain strength, I unwrapped two of the rolled leaves and ate the stick of rice paste and slurped down the too hot tea. Afterwards I crawled back into the heavy underbrush, curled up in my orange robe and was asleep in minutes.

I slept right near my raft and woke with the first light. By searching down river for a short distance I was able to find a downed tree that I hacked and scraped until it resembled a crude log boat. I hoped to use it not just to keep me afloat, but stow my pack in a relatively dry and secure way. After tying it to the smaller tree, I took off the orange robe, and put on my camouflaged pattern pants and shirt. With one last long look in the direction of the monastery, I pushed the raft into the water and held on. The current grabbed the raft, and moved me quickly east and south. I hoisted myself aboard and let the river take me away.

All day, I drifted. I was afraid to move too near the shore because the area seemed too populated. I steered towards the middle and drifted past many rice farms and some pole huts. I counted nine sightings of locals. Most all wore the traditional black that the Viet Cong had adapted as their uniform. Luckily, no one even glanced in my direction.

About dusk I heard the putt-putt of a small boat. I turned my raft so that I was closer to the shore, and the branches of my tree separated me from the middle of the river. After about five minutes of worry, an old boat chugged past. Three men talked idly and paid no attention to my raft, although I could see the ever-present AK-47s propped against the cabin.

When it was fully dark I edged towards a sand bar and grounded the raft. I was nearly too tired to stand, but for sure too waterlogged to stay in the water. I managed to drag the raft onto the bank and up under the trees that lined the river.

I scouted in both directions, but there were no pole huts to be seen. I unwrapped my orange robe and used it as a blanket. After I took a long drink from the canteen I lay back against the log boat and slept without eating.

As was my habit I awakened before first light. I dreamed I heard the gong of the monastery and opened my eyes and was surprised to see that I had made my bed right near a rice paddy. I did my best to conceal the evidence of my resting place and quickly pushed off into the river, fearful that an early morning farmer might see me and sound the alarm. I managed to find some spicy vegetables the monks had wrapped in leaves, and munched on them as I floated.

I closed my eyes for a moment to silently bless the monks as I floated through the countryside. No sooner had I closed my eyes than I heard the soft voice of Beloved Abbot, "Remember to embrace each moment with gratitude, Brother Toby, for the one thing we actually can all control is our attitude."

I shook my head, trying to jar the voices from my consciousness. I needed to keep my wits if I was to survive where everyone I encountered seemed to be the enemy.

I had plenty of time to think as I drifted. I thought about the kindness of the monks. I grinned at the idea that I had tried so carefully to hide my intentions from them. They must have known my every thought. Again the memory of the voice of the Abbot sounded inside my head. "If we remember to listen within, we will discover that there is but one mind, and it remains accessible to anyone who stills his mind enough to hear it."

And so I floated. I floated towards each new moment. I tried to remember to "embrace..." each new scene that unfolded as I drifted. Each turn in the river brought a new and different sight. The people became less frequent, but water snakes seemed to show up more often. Most were poisonous, and I avoided them when I could. I tried to remember to bless those snakes like the monks would, but when one swam too close I just held the K-bar in my hand and held my breath until the snake lost interest and swam away.

That night, I beached the raft right at the first hint of darkness, pulling again under the canopy of trees. I took my time and carefully scouted the area. There was no sign of huts or rice fields, so I returned and made a small fire and sipped a wonderful cup of tea. My evening meal consisted of some rice, two spicy radishes and a manioc.

I wondered how many miles I had traveled from the monastery as I made my bed. I noticed that the river had become much larger through the day, and the flow of the river had slowed, meaning that the countryside was less hilly.

Making my bed in the log boat, I crawled in

and pulled the orange robe over my shoulders and slept.

Again, I woke up at first light. I was stiff and sore from the cramped bed in the raft, but very hungry. I searched the pack and found enough wrapped rice and hot radishes to ease the hunger. I drained the first canteen, and made a mental note to boil extra water tonight to refill it. I slipped the orange robe on and stashed the army uniform as cargo for another day on the water, making sure to tie it all securely.

I pushed on the raft to shove it back into the water, but it had become lodged in the sandbar. I had to squat and lift with my legs to free it. The first attempt I slipped, but the second try propelled it into the water. It moved rapidly away from me.

I turned to grab my machete and remaining canteen, and looked directly into the muzzle of an AK-47. A skinny man, about my age or a little older, looked at me with an unreadable expression. His brown eyes told me nothing, but there was just a smattering of freckles across his nose. His black pajamas showed sweat stains beneath the armpits.

He placed the barrel sight under my chin and pressed upwards. I had no choice but to stand erect. I forgot for an instant about my bad foot, and put my weight on it. The sharp pain took me by surprise and nearly made me pass out. I glanced downward and could see that the machete less than two feet away, but he saw it too and moved the weapon and my chin away from it.

Out of the corner of my eye I could see my raft as the current took it away. I remember thinking that everything I owned was on my body or in that raft.

I remembered that I still had the K-bar knife slipped under the sash in the middle of my back. I knew I couldn't grab it before he could pull the trigger, but it was still reassuring to know it was back there.

"Turn around slowly," the man said in passable English. I swallowed and slowly turned, and felt the knife being removed. Now the barrel of the weapon prodded me to move. "To the right," came the terse command. I veered right and found a trail. My foot hurt with each step, but he seemed in a big hurry.

"Step faster or I will bury you right here."

I tried to move faster, but the pain and now the soggy bandage wouldn't allow it. "If I go any faster, I'll bleed to death, and you will have to bury me here. Can't you see my foot and ankle?"

There was no reply, but I thought I noticed a slight easing of the pressure of the weapon in by back.

We climbed a gentle hill and entered into a more forested area. Soon I could see two thatched roof huts. We passed the first and continued towards the second. In front of a red plywood door I was ordered to stop. My captor called out for the occupant, but no one came.

He ordered me to sit down where I stood and produced a rusty key. Holding the weapon less than three inches from my nose, he managed to use his other hand to open a tiny padlock on the front door. He kept his weapon in my direction and disappeared for a moment inside. When he came out he was frowning.

The door of the other hut banged open and two older men appeared. When they saw me sitting on the ground, and the freckle-faced guy pointing his weapon at me, they came quickly over. Both were also carrying AK-47s.

They came right up to me and put their faces real close to mine, studying my face and the orange robe. The smaller one had a large scar that zigzagged across his face from his left ear to a spot under his left eye.

"He's a long nose," The scar guy said. "Let's kill him now!" He raised his weapon but the freckle-faced guy pointed his own gun directly at the scar. In Vietnamese he said, "Shoot him, and you die with him."

I'm sure that they had no idea that I could understand them, but it sure made me wonder why freckle-face was protecting me. The older one stood impassively to one side. For a minute it looked like a Mexican standoff, but finally scar lowered his weapon. Without warning he spit right in my face. I tried not to react, but could feel the wetness as it seeped down my face.

My captor ordered them both to pack for a long hike. The older one bowed and left, but scar scowled. "Kill him now. At least that will avenge my wife. If you let me cut his throat, then her spirit can be at peace."

"Uncle Ho will deal with the long-nose. Maybe he has information. It is not up to us to decide. We follow orders, right, comrade?"

Uncle Ho was an obvious reference to Ho Chi Minh, and to use his name was to appeal to an unquestioned authority. Scar scowled and made a very cursory bow. "I shall first bury my wife, and then I will join you at the camp." He spit again on my cheek and turned and walked away without looking back. This time I pretended it didn't happen.

The older man returned with a black backpack and his weapon slung across his shoulder. He walked right up to me and kicked me fully in the stomach. I cried out and doubled up in agony. I rolled over and tried to stand, but passed out as the flow of blood stained my robe.

A splash of water in my face brought me back awake, and in English I was ordered to stand. It took a minute, and it hurt like hell. Freckle-face untied my robe and stared at the purple and red wound on my mid-section, which now seeped blood.

"Get a first-aid kit now!" freckle-face ordered. You

have always had a way of making a mission more difficult!" The older guy scowled and ran back to his hut.

Moments later he reappeared with U.S Army field Medical kit. He opened it and found the Iodine and poured it right onto my wound.

I gasped and willed myself not to cry out as the searing bite of the iodine hit. Before I could even catch my breath he covered the wound with a large gauze bandage and was ripping strips of tape and pressing them to my belly. He applied them right across the wound, not to the sides.

He stood and surveyed his work like a first year med student. I held my hand over the wound, trying not to disturb it too much as I struggled again to my feet.

The three of us left the village and walked uphill, away from the river. We trudged along for about an hour, gaining altitude with nearly every step. My foot was a filthy mixture of blood and sweat and dust. Neither of my captors seemed the least bit sympathetic.

At the top of a rise, we paused, overlooking a valley filled with terraced rice paddies. The sun was incredibly hot, my foot was throbbing and bleeding, and my belly was feeling like I'd been poked with a hot branding iron. I thought I heard Truong's voice inside my head. ""Embrace each moment as if it were your last."

I smiled grimly, and thought, "Thanks a bunch,

Brother Truong."

Prodded by the barrel of a weapon, we descended to a large hut beside a submerged rice paddy. By the time we got there a crowd had gathered. A large and mangy yellow and brown dog lunged at my bleeding foot, and freckle face slammed the stock of his weapon against its jaw with such force that it yelped and slunk away.

If that dog was someone's pet, they didn't love it enough to challenge my captor's actions. He spoke with authority, and ordered that I be placed in a jail, which turned out to be a room in the large building that had a lock. I was too tired to try to escape anyway, but didn't want to tell them that. I found some old sacks in the corner and fashioned a bed.

Much later my captor unlocked the door and handed me two turnips and three radishes and two small rolled leafs filled with rice. He waited silently while I ate.

"Hold your bowl still, and I'll pour some tea," he said in English. After he poured, I said, "Thank you."

He nodded at my midsection, "Is that a gunshot wound in your belly?"

"**No,** it's from a tree branch."

His face showed disbelief. "A tree branch? How did it occur?"

I smiled and said in Vietnamese, "An artillery round exploded and propelled me into a tree.

May I know your name?"

That got a reaction from him. He grimaced, but quickly replaced his surprise with the poker face I'd seen earlier. He stared at my belly for a long time before speaking.

"You would be dead if that were true," he said in English.

I had to smile. "That is what the monks who rescued me said, too. They sewed me up and put medicine on the wounds. "

"They should have let you die," he said.

He studied me for a moment before walking out and locking the door.

The next day I didn't even hear him unlock the door. I awakened when he shook my shoulder. "Get up! Eat quickly. We have a long walk today."

I found the food he had left and wolfed it down. When I pushed the plywood door open he was standing in the path, his weapon resting in the crook of his arm. The other older man who had been with us yesterday was nowhere in sight. It was still dark when the two of us set out. Most of the village was just starting to stir.

I stepped onto the path in front of him and we headed west, up yet one more steep hill. With my sore belly and my sore foot we didn't make good time. I could tell that my captor was losing his patience, but my stamina was not at its best. I kept expecting a shove, or an order to hurry, but it didn't come.

We walked for hours, up one hill, down the other side, and up yet another. I was starting to falter when he finally commanded me to halt. The sun was directly overhead, and incredibly hot. I wished I had my old brimmed field hat to protect my shaved head.

I sat down in the shade of a huge tree. He took a long swig from a canteen, probably mine, and offered it to me. I drank deeply, not minding that the water was warm. I rested for about twenty minutes before he ordered me up and away, with no mention of food.

We walked all day, taking only that one break. I really worked at not slowing him down. I used a method the Abbot had discussed where you imagine that you are not in the body, but floating above it and observing without any judgment. It worked for a while, but then I tripped on a hidden root, and went sprawling on my face. As I lay there with my mouth full of dirt, and blood spurting from my bum ankle, I could hear the Abbot's voice, "Embrace each moment," I imagined embracing the mud in my mouth. Just then freckle-face said, "Let's take a rest. I sighed and fell asleep where I lay.

Pain in my foot awakened me, and I opened my eyes to see my captor washing my wound. He refused to make eye contact with me, but placed a dark green leaf directly on the wound. He then went about applying a clean dressing. "That will draw out the infection," he said. I was too sore and too tired to care. He looked around and spoke, almost facing the trees instead of me. "This is a good place for a camp."

He set about making a fire, not even bothering to try to hide it. I drifted off to sleep and awakened in the darkness. He was sitting near me smoking a cigarette.

I rolled over and tried to sit up. He made no move for his weapon, but watched me struggle until I managed to get my feet fully situated. He got up and went to the fire-pit and brought back a piece of roasted meat.

I had not had any meat since being brought to the temple by the monks, and I just stared at it. The local populations seemed okay with roasted dog, cat, or even rat. I wasn't sure which of these it was, or if I should even care. I was just about to reach for it when he pulled it away.

He said, "Buddhists don't eat meat, but I thought I would check." I swallowed, and asked him if he had any rice or vegetables. He chewed slowly on the piece of meat. When he finished, he went again to the fire and brought my bowl filled with orange radishes and white rice. I thanked him and ate in silence while he watched me eat.

The next day about noon we came to another village. A cry went up as we approached, and a crowd gathered. Armed boys with ancient rifles escorted us to the middle of the clearing. Old women shouted and spit and cursed me. He barked an order and they dropped back.

An old man with a huge and ancient rifle screamed something I couldn't understand. He raised it to his shoulder, but before he could pull the trigger my captor wrenched it from his hands. He tried to kick me but was shoved backwards, landing in a heap. He got up slowly and turned his back and walked away. It looked like everyone in the village wanted me dead.

After much shouting and talking, a rope was placed around my middle and I was led to a pit and shoved in. It was at least eight feet deep, and I tumbled headfirst. The village cheered and made high-pitched noises. Many spit, and some threw rocks.

I managed to reposition myself with my feet below my head and looked up and saw two men place a heavy steel grate over the top. They laughed and spit before they left.

The ground smelled of urine, and the pit was damp. I moved back and forth, trying to find a position that didn't hurt too much. When they dug the hole it was about four feet across, but got smaller as it got deeper. I found myself wedged tightly into a narrow part at the bottom of the hole. I looked around and said to the darkness, "Embrace this, Beloved Abbot!"

I sat there, too numb to even think for some

time. Finally, I heard a movement outside, and a wrinkled old woman with blackened teeth appeared and got down on her hands and knees. She squinted through the bars until she spotted me. "You killed my sons!" she croaked.

I wanted to tell her that I had never even been in this village, but it didn't seem like it would make any difference to her, so I just stared back at her. She stood up and pulled down her black pajama pants and squatted on the grate. A torrent of urine rained down on me. She redressed and kneeled again. "I hope you die tonight," she yelled.

I quickly realized that I couldn't hold my breath forever, and decided to risk a small breath. The pungent odor nearly gagged me. The words of my first sergeant popped into my mind, "I just don't get any better than this, eh?"

I huddled there in my piss-soaked robe in the cold and damp ground and asked myself why I ever wanted to leave the safety and serenity of the temple.

Truong's voice answered my question inside my mind. We had once been talking about destiny and fate. He was explaining one of the Abbot's lectures.

"We would like to think we have free will, but it is possible that everything we do is predetermined by our intentions. Once our intentions are clear, we find ourselves impelled to action."

I sighed and wondered if I was going insane.

Hearing voices was a sign of losing your sanity, wasn't it? I was tired enough that I soon fell asleep crouching there.

I woke up at the first hint of light, stiff and sore. My foot hurt with a numbing throb. I tried to stand, but there just wasn't enough room for both feet. The sore one couldn't hold the weight, and the other one was too cramped to be of any use.

I was afraid that if I got my knees to bend I would be wedged in, so I just made the best of it and leaned my head back and closed my eyes, trying to think.

I wondered what kind of advice the Abbot would offer in this sort of a situation. "When no course of action presents itself, the wise man meditates."

That fast, the thought sprang forth in my mind in the Abbot's soft voice. I even thought I heard Truong snicker in the background.

"Wow," I muttered. "I'm starting to hallucinate!"

My mind seemed restless, so I closed my eyes and started the process of noticing my breath. The Abbot taught me to "Breathe in the pain of the world, embrace it and bless it as a teacher. Then breathe out a blessing for all the suffering souls."

"Suffering souls," I mused. "Here I am halfway around the world from everything I know and love. All the men in my unit are dead. I haven't seen or spoken to another American in God knows how long. My current living quarters is the bottom of a piss-filled pit somewhere above the DMZ that the villagers use as a latrine. And, oh yeah! They all want to kill me! Does this qualify as a suffering soul?"

I closed my eyes even tighter and tried to imagine the face of the old Abbot. "How would you respond to that one, old buddy?

"What is the first of the Four Noble Truths? Brother Toby?" It really was the Abbot's soft voice inside my head; with the same rhythm to his sing-song voice. Could it be that those monks had some clairvoyant way of communicating?

Again the question came. This time the voice sounded a little more insistent. "Okay, sure. All life is suffering. But some suffer more than others. And yes, I know that all suffering can be alleviated. That's the second one."

"Well," said the Abbot's voice with more than a little humor. "Then you know the drill."

They had gently chided me when I called the eightfold path the drill. Basically, there were eight attitudes that the monks tried to maintain. Each one supposedly lead to the next, starting with right understanding. If we had a right understanding of the big picture, it would lead to right thinking, and from that would come right speech, which would demand right action, etc.

Although the concepts were by now familiar, I was having trouble applying them to my situation. Basically I wondered how all this could get me out of the damp pit.

So often right action to a Buddhist was simply to tune out the outer world and listen within. That's what they called meditating. My dad was fond of saying that it was hard to remember that we came to drain a swamp when we were up to our asses in alligators. But the Abbot said that when nothing else presented itself as a course of action, we could sleep and remain in the problem, or we could meditate.

So I closed my eyes again and tried to return to the meditation. I breathed in all the pain, and devoured it into my heart, and transformed its energy into blessings and tried to send it out into the world.

Now Truong's voice spoke to me as he translated and explained the Abbot's teaching. "It is neither our pain nor their pain. It is just universal suffering. It is impersonal and it will land on all of us."

I continued the breathing exercise, trying to remember what came next. "It's not the suffering, but our resistance to it that causes us misery."

Resistance? How could anyone not resist living in the latrine? I heard a sound, and my eyes popped open. In the early morning light a small girl's face appeared. She was maybe five or six and she was on her hands and knees. Dark brown eyes looked down on me. She greeted me in Vietnamese, and I answered her back.

"Are you hungry?" she asked in a stage whisper. "Yes," I croaked. Her tiny hand thrust a package through the iron grate. It looked like a leaf, all wadded up, and it slipped from her hand and fell to the bottom of the pit. "Oh, I'm so sorry," she said.

I stooped and groped with my right hand, and found it wedged against my knee. I held it up to her and said, "Don't be sorry, I found it. Thank you." She studied me for just an instant and flashed a tiny smile, and was gone. I unwrapped the leaf and there was a small quantity of rice, and a small red pepper. I started to stuff it into my mouth, but remembered what the monks taught.

"Eat slowly, focusing your entire being and attention on what you are eating. Fill your mind with gratitude, and accept it as a blessing for all beings. Savor each morsel."

So I put a small amount of the rice in my mouth and sucked all the juice from it, and chewed it into a paste before swallowing it.

Each bite took about a minute, and I managed to make the gift last for several minutes. When it was all gone I popped the hot pepper into my mouth and said aloud, "Best meal I ever ate!"

"And maybe your last." said a voice from the grate. A freckled face appeared above my head.

"Where did you learn your English?" I asked.

He disappeared without answering, and then I heard the sound of metal on metal, and soon the grate was raised and set aside. He pushed a long piece of angle iron at me and said, "Grab it, and I will help pull you out."

I did, and he did. Soon I lay panting on the ground at the edge of the pit.

He tossed the iron aside and picked up his AK-47, pointing it at me. "Time to go," he said in a near monotone.

The sun was just about to appear, but still below the horizon, making the eastern sky glow in the darkness. I got to my feet and felt the barrel poking into my back. We headed for the jungle again. I was still hungry, but apparently breakfast had already been served.

"Just keep moving," he ordered.

It was again uphill most of the day. I had the sinking sensation of walking right back to where I had started, but knew I was heading as much north as west.

We walked all day, and the jungle thinned and changed to a sparse forest, with occasional open meadows. We walked all day and never encountered another soul. Outcropping rocks began to appear, as we followed a well-worn path.

By early afternoon, my foot was throbbing and a bloody mess. I struggled to be able to simply pick it up and let it fall, emptying my mind of everything but that simple task of picking up my feet and placing them in front of me.

Finally the order to stop came. I crumpled

immediately to the ground, trying to elevate the sore foot. I managed to fling it up on a fallen tree.

"A walking stick or crutch would help me walk," I said. My captor just glared at me and rummaged in his backpack. "Are we in Laos yet," I asked.

He met my question with an icy stare. "Do not speak unless you are spoken to," he ordered. He reached into his pack and got a coarse rope and made a loop in one end. He tied my feet and then my hands. Sensing that the time for conversation had past, I closed my eyes. I was almost instantly asleep.

When I woke up, there was a crude crutch next to me. I looked at him to thank him but he turned away. "Eat fast," he said, "you can make up for how slow you walk!"

He untied me and I struggled to my feet. I tried a couple of steps with the crutch. I could see an improvement almost immediately, as it allowed me to use my sore foot without placing full weight on it.

We walked uphill and westward for most of the morning at a fast pace. Three times he thought he heard something and we got quickly off the trail and hid in the deep underbrush. I didn't see anyone, but my captor was taking no chances. I could always hope it was ARVN or American troops, but I never saw anyone at all.

Just before midday the trail leveled and then

started going downhill. I figured this guy must have been planning to meet up with someone, and was running late. We never did have lunch or even stop except for a quick sip of water. I was so glad we were finally going downhill that I forgot to be worried that we were getting closer to what might be a POW camp.

Suddenly he poked me roughly in the middle of my back and hissed to me to hide. l ducked behind a huge tree trunk ,with him right behind me. Maybe three seconds later, five men came into view. They were unkempt and smelled strongly of body odor. But the most interesting thing was their hair. Each one had long hair, longer than most Asian women wear it. Each was carrying a weapon, and they were trotting. They trotted right past us heading the same direction we were going.

"Cambodians!" my captor whispered. "They would kill both of us if they saw us."

"We are still in Viet Nam," he answered to the question I was going to ask. "They kill everyone they meet, even their own people."

I opened my mouth to speak but he shushed me. Just then seven more came trotting by. My captor pulled on my robe and I backed away from the trail. We worked carefully to get through the heavy underbrush without making noise, and came at last to a large tree with dense branches and leaves. He pulled aside one of the branches and shoved me in front of him.

I looked around at an open area that was completely hidden from the outside. It looked as though it might even keep the rain off of us. "We make camp here... no fire," he said.

I wondered if he was going to tie my hands and feet, but he just laid his pack down and searched its contents. I was tired enough that I sat cross-legged on the soft grass. I wondered how grass could grow where no sun ever reached. But I was too tired to think. I watched passively as he divided the remaining ration of rice into two nearly equal parts and covered each with pieces of cabbage. He handed one to me and we ate in silence.

My habit was to chew each bite completely and savor the tastes. He ate absent-mindedly, and finished before I was halfway. A swallow each from a canteen and we were out of water. He made a pillow of his pack and lay down on his back. His weapon was near his right hand. "Don't even think of leaving," he warned. "You would be caught and killed in a slow and cruel way." Then he closed his eyes.

I finished my meal and wondered if he was asleep or just closing his eyes. Either way I didn't plan on leaving and ending up with the Cambodians. I straightened my spine and started my breathing exercises.

I must have sat there for hours. The sun went down, and the dark night crept in. It became so totally dark under that canopy that I am not sure I could have seen my hand if I held it in front of my nose.

Thoughts of other camps arose. I recalled the last night with my unit, and the excitement of preparing for a last mission. Then the nights in the temple appeared in my mind. I noticed them, but didn't attach to them. Next came thoughts of the Abbot, and Truong, and the long discussions in the temple. Each time I simply noticed without any grasping or clinging. Each thought sort of softened and then vanished, and it seemed to take longer and longer for another to appear.

There seemed to be a long time between each breath too, and yet I stayed comfortable, watching as a small point of light inside my head seemed to get brighter and closer.

This too I noticed without putting any significance on it. It was almost like I was too tired to care what appeared within my mind. The light moved closer and closer still, and brighter too. I began to wonder if it could be seen, so I opened my eyes.

The entire scene was actually glowing, not from any external source of light, but from itself. The ground glowed brightly. My captor seemed to radiate light, and even the weapon glowed with a light all its' own. My feet, my knees, everything! It all glowed. The tree, the branches above. The leaves. Everything I saw was pulsating light. I wondered briefly if I was going blind, and rubbed my eyes with my glowing hand. I held it out at arm's length and turned it palm up, then palm down. It didn't seem to matter which way I turned it or where I placed it. It all glowed and pulsated. I closed my eyes and the glow remained, but inside of me there seemed not to be any shapes, just light.

Now I heard the soft voice of the Abbot. "Embrace this too, Toby." His sing-song voice sounded clearly as if he were very close to me. "You are not dreaming now. Maybe for the second time in your life you are awake beyond the dream.

Embrace it all, Brother Toby. And try to recall this moment when you get really lost in the dream."

I scarcely dared to breathe. It was so beautiful that I wanted to hold the light in my mind forever. But even as I looked about the campsite, I saw the light fading. Too soon the pitch darkness surrounded me.

I sighed, and wondered what was real. I stood up and stretched in the pitch darkness, and groped around until I found a comfortable place to lie down to sleep. I could hear my captor snoring softly somewhere nearby.

Chapter 6

I dreamed again of mail call back at base camp. I could hear the "pop-pop" of the Huey and the sounds of the soldiers' feet as they ran to the landing zone.

The coming of the mailbag was always a time of high interest to the guys. I ran too, even though I knew that I would get a letter from Myrna.

I dreamed this dream so many times I knew how it would go. I knew I would get an envelope, to open it and read that Myrna was marrying a hippie.

The crazy part was that although I knew how it was going to go, I would keep hoping that this time I could make the dream end differently. And so I would stand around with all the other guys, and wait, and hope that there was no letter for me.

But there always was. And it never changed. It always had her childish handwriting with the little round circles above each "i" and the short and low crossings of each "t."

Each time it started the same way. "Dear Toby," it began. "I hope you are doing okay." I didn't need to read the rest, because I knew it was going to tell me that she was marrying a guy named Ted from Kent State.

Myrna even said in the letter that I would like this guy if I got to know him.

Fat chance! I always crumpled up the letter after she wrote that. But this time I willed myself to change the dream. So instead of burning the letter in the ashtray, I willed myself to see it folded and put it in my footlocker. And so I was able to change the dream.

For the first time I was actually a little glad that our engagement was over. And it helped me to become aware that I really wasn't sure I was the same guy she kissed goodbye at the airport. And I wasn't sure that I even knew her well enough to marry her. And this time, I actually smiled at the idea that I might like Ted. Hell, I probably would, if I ever met him. I would shake his hand and introduce myself, "I'm the guy from her hometown, her childhood sweetheart. Pleased to meet you."

I recalled that our letters had started out so passionate, so honest. But as the months passed, they got more polite, less revealing. After the fourth month neither of us really talked about our deepest thoughts or our daydreams.

So this time, in this dream, I blessed her and wished her well, and Ted too. For the first time I saw her as if we were two ships, each heading in a different direction, which just happened to share some space for a moment before they passed out of sight.

It was then that I realized that her last few letters weren't even signed with love, just her name at the bottom of the page.

I woke up in total darkness of the night, moved by a deep sense of peacefulness. My captor slept, snoring lightly. There was no way to tell what time it was. But I was completely awake so I sat up and made myself comfortable.

The first thought I had was a vivid memory of watching the raft with all my possessions float down the river. The next one was a sense of lightness; of being freer than I had ever remembered being.

I smiled as I realized that I had originally resisted the Abbot's idea that a monk needs only a bowl, a robe and sandals. I thought about my pocket bible, knowing full well I couldn't have even seen it in the pre-dawn darkness. Did I miss it because I believed it had protected me? Or did I miss its wisdom?

I tried to remember some of my favorite

passages. All I could think of was the story about the people who met Jesus, and they turned away,

"I was cold, and you didn't offer me a coat. I was hungry, and you didn't share your meal." And one of them said, "But Master, we didn't recognize you!" And he answered and said, "What so ever you do unto the least of them, you do unto me."

One of the Abbot's lectures talked about the concept of right timing. He had said that everything that seems to occur in our lives happens at exactly the moment when it will be in our best interest. "Accidents are only possible in our perception, but impossible in the grand scheme of things."

So why had the thought of this parable occurred to me tonight? Was it just because it was the first thing I could remember? It didn't actually seem to apply in my current situation; at least not to me.

If my sleeping captor had heard it, I am sure it would have had some significance. But I was his captive, in a hostile land, held against my will in a place very near Cambodia. And the worst part was, my captor seemed like the better of two awful choices.

"Breathe in the suffering," came the voice of the old Abbot. "Embrace it all, and let it into your heart. Transform it to a blessing and send it out to everyone.

Exclude no one. Send it to all sentient beings."

It seemed as though the Abbot had his own key to get into my head, and there was little I could do to stop him, so I just let him ramble.

He continued. "Loving-kindness is not real until it is offered to everyone indiscriminately. Can you offer loving kindness?"

In the temple, each monk would respond with an affirmative, "Of course!" Almost before I thought about it, I said it aloud.

My captor stirred, sighing deeply and softly whimpered in the darkness nearby.

I asked myself if I could bless this man who kept poking me with a loaded weapon. "Of course I can," came my silent reply.

Next came the vision of Myrna's soft brown hair. In the summers it looked blonde, but by winter it was a light brown. Her smile could still light up a dark night. Could I bless her? "Of course!"

That old woman who appeared above me in the pit showed up next. I could see the hatred in her face, and I closed my eyes as the thought of her urinating all over me. Her too? I winced when I thought of her.

Could I honestly offer her a blessing? I wondered what kind of a life she had in a small village. I wondered if she had watched her husband die. ARVN and American troops often visited the villages randomly, and any sudden move might result in a shooting.

And after dark, the Viet Cong appeared. Any sign of hesitancy or even an implied unwillingness to support the cause could have ended in a death at the hands of the VC.

Maybe she had lost children, or grandchildren. How could I possibly know her mind?

"You can't," came the voice of Beloved Abbot. "But you can bless her and hold her in loving kindness in your mind." I sighed, "Of course I can," I said finally.

The faces changed from Vietnamese to American, from old to young. I saw the men of my unit. I silently blessed each one. I saw the face of my Commanding Officer. I even saw the face of that Lieutenant who just had to go on our last patrol.

I wondered if he had a wife who got a visit from the Chaplain and another officer. I wondered if he had kids.

The blessings came easier now. And the last face that appeared was a young soldier that at first I didn't even recognize.

"It is you, Brother Toby!" came the voice of Truong. I winced at the size of the crowd that seemed to be gathering in my head, and took another look at the face. Yep. It was a younger version of myself. So I blessed that image too.

I spent the night sitting in the lotus pose. I blessed everyone that came to mind. I even blessed the politicians on both sides of this crazy war, the hippies that protested the war, and the South

Vietnamese officers who made sure they were never anywhere near the front.

I found myself letting go of all the grievances I had held against anyone or any group. For a fleeting instance, I even saw the faces of those Cambodians with the long hair that my captor seemed so intent on avoiding. I sent them a blessing just in case.

The light of dawn came upon me as I sat. I watched the jungle stir and awaken. I saw tiny critters on the earthen floor of the forest as they got themselves busy doing what they do. A couple of ants checked my foot out, but as I blasted them with loving-kindness they turned away.

I watched my captor sleeping, knowing that I could easily have grabbed his weapon and made him my captive. But there didn't seem to be any reason to disturb the order of it all. Soon enough he opened his eyes.

When he saw me sitting there he quickly sat up and grabbed the weapon. A look of surprise flicked across his face for an instant, only to be replaced by the stoic mask.

"We must leave immediately," he said in English.

When I didn't respond, he jumped to his feet and pointed the weapon at me. "Get on your feet now!" he ordered.

I struggled to my feet, stiff and sore from a whole night in the lotus pose. I had to test each leg and massage the circulation back to be able to feel anything. He watched impassively.

"A change of plans?" I asked.

"Cambodians are not supposed to be in Viet Nam. I must get word of this to my superiors. We leave immediately."

I nodded and grabbed my crutch and gear. We walked back the way we had come, with the morning sun in our eyes and the fear of an encounter keeping us next to one side of the trail. We walked uphill most of the day. Twice we jumped into the forest, once to watch three Cambodians heading west, and once to watch an old farmer lugging rice sacks tied on a pole across his shoulders.

The trail started to look familiar, and I knew we would soon be stopping, since I remembered a group of trees that signaled the nearby presence of a small river. We had made camp on the other side, and he had dug up two maniocs and replanted the seeds.

We forded the stream and he ordered me off the trail. I smiled to see his garden.

"We should be safe here," he said. He set about making a small fire. I watched as he made a circle of rocks, just like my dad had taught me so many years ago on our camping trips back in Oklahoma. He dug through his pack and produced an old aluminum coffeepot, which he filled with canteen water and placed in the fire.

Next to it he placed a pan, with its handle missing, into the coals, and splashed a small amount of water into it.

My captor took his time fixing vegetables and rice, and even dug in his pack and came up with some garlic. The tea was nice and hot and smelled like good green tea. He handed me a full bowl of food and left the fire going. I figured he must have felt he was in a very safe part of the country.

I bowed when he handed the steaming bowl to me, mostly out of a habit I hadn't realized I had formed from my stay at the temple. He bowed in return, and we both sat and ate in silence.

I had given up on asking him any questions, and vowed that I would only respond when he spoke. He seemed more than okay with that. The evening grew later and the fire burned down, and still he made no effort to douse it, or hide it, or disguise our campsite.

I had the feeling that we had pretty much arrived at wherever we were heading, with him getting careless with the campsite. My suspicions were confirmed when he produced a cigarette and lit up. He offered me one, but I waived it away.

I ate slowly as he inhaled deeply and let the smoke cascade out of his slightly opened mouth. He seemed to be studying me as intently as I studied him.

"You eat too slow," he said.

I nodded. "You told me that before. And I told

you that you eat too fast, remember?"

He nodded and pinched out the cigarette. He carefully placed the remainder in his shirt pocket and stood up. "It's time for the rope," he said.

I set my bowl and cup to the side and stood up, thinking he was going to tie my legs again. He busied himself with the rope and secured my hands in front of me and then threw dirt over the fire and stomped out any embers. Without another word he lay down next to the ever-present AK-47 and closed his eyes.

"Goodnight," I called. He didn't answer. "I'd hate to meet you in a poker game," I said, more to myself than to him.

Without moving in the darkness, a voice from his direction said, "You would lose."

I smiled and yawned and realized how tired I was. With my hands tied I couldn't even wash out the cup and bowl, so I lay on my back and closed my eyes and was instantly asleep.

The whistle of incoming artillery came in the dead of night. I may have awakened with the first round fired, and the soldier in me sensed that there was trouble. I was on my feet when the first explosion hit about two hundred feet from us, and directly in the middle of the path we had walked earlier.

I heard the whistle of the next round and broke into a full run. My captor passed me running fast, but he didn't have the handicap of tied hands. The moon was up, and finding the trail was not difficult. I watched his dark figure disappear into the dark shadows in front of me.

A huge explosion behind me spurred me into even more speed, and I ran for my life. The trouble is my bad leg was slowing me down, and those shells were being walked right at my position. I veered left, off the trail and into the heavy undergrowth. I could hear the boots of my captor, and knew that he had also left the trail and was somewhere in front of me. I tripped and slammed my face first into the muddy ground with a thud.

The shrill whistle of the incoming round sounded much too close, so I closed my eyes. I would have covered my head, if my hands weren't tied, but I pressed my face deeper into the mud.

Even with eyes tightly closed and filled with mud I could see the brilliant flash in front of me light up the jungle, with a deafening explosion that followed a millisecond later. Shrapnel whistled past me just inches above my head. "Oh, God!" I called into the mud and the darkness.

The explosion in front of me was exactly where I had heard the thrashing and running of my captor. I managed to jump to my feet and run towards the mayhem in front of me, cursing the idiot who had tied me.

"Are you all right?" I called into the darkness. I

was running as fast as I could go when my head whacked into a huge low-hanging branch, hitting me just above the eyes. I slammed to the earth again. "Oh, shit." I muttered just before I lost consciousness.

A strange tickling sensation brought me awake in the full of the day. The sunlight burned my muddy eyes and I blinked and squinted, trying to see in the glare. I finally managed to open one eye and began blinking rapidly, trying to focus.

The strange shape of a furry face with long whiskers and beady black eyes formed in my vision. It was less than an inch from my nose, and smelled like death in a sewer. A mouth opened, revealing filthy pointed teeth and a gut wrenching case of bad breath. The stench shocked me fully awake, and I sat bolt upright, slamming my forehead into a giant black rodent's snout.

A strange and guttural scream arose from deep within me, and was instantly matched by a high-pitched howl from the rat. It sprang backwards and hissed.

Somehow, without the use of my hands, I was on my feet. I kicked wildly at the startled rat, got lucky and caught him on the snout. He squealed and flew backwards hitting a tree. He landed with a thud, obviously stunned for an instant, but was up quickly and scurried away. I looked around wildly, fearful that there were more of these giant rats, but he must have been alone.

Panting and gasping, I leaned forward and vomited again and again.

When there was no more to eject, and my stomach was contorted in pain, I fell on my knees and cried for a long time. The sobbing finally stopped and I stood and backed away from the stench of my own vomit. My memory kicked in and I recalled the horror of the night.

It didn't take any effort to find his trail, and follow it through the jungle. I must have trailed him for two or three minutes before I came to a huge crater. Off to the left and outside the crater I spotted the crumpled body, face down in a pool of blood. My K-bar knife was visible tucked into the back of his belt.

It took me a couple of minutes to hobble around the edge of the crater. When I got to the body I used my good foot to nudge his body. There was no response. The amount of blood suggested that if he wasn't dead now, he would be shortly. Since he had tied my hands in front of me it took only a few tries to remove the K-bar knife from his belt. I swatted several times at the flies with the knife. I guess I thought that maybe I could cut one of those flies with the knife? I smiled at the absurdity of it and quit trying to disturb the flies and focused on freeing my hands.

I dropped the knife twice before I managed to cut the cotton rope from my wrists. He had tied it so tightly that I had to rub my wrists to regain circulation.

A soft moan from the crumpled form jerked my head around, so I hurried over and heaved him over on his back and probed for a pulse. I didn't find any on the wrist, but detected a very faint one on his neck. It was there, but it was weak. Real weak.

I pulled and tugged until I had removed him from the pool of blood. His right trouser was soaked from the knee down. I used the K-bar and sliced away his pant leg, revealing a huge chunk of blackened steel that was imbedded in his shinbone. The tendons on the front sides of his leg had been severed, and the foot flopped wildly when I attempted to reposition the leg. I started to work quickly with the knife, and the shrapnel piece gave way.

I grabbed it and tossed it aside. "It won't take long to amputate this one," I said to the unconscious form in front of me. "The artillery shell did most of the work.

I didn't have anything to deaden the pain, and knew I had to saw through the shin-bone, so I figured that if I kept talking, it might distract him. I watched to see if he would scream or pull away as I used the serrated part of the blade. He never moved.

I had seen two other battlefield surgeries, and was basically faking it and trying to sound and seem like I knew what I was doing. But I knew that if I didn't perform the surgery now, he would never live long enough to do it later. Hell, he was nearly dead as it was.

I cut the remaining dangling tendons, completely freeing the foot and a small portion of the ankle. I left a long flap of skin to wrap over the stub, wrapped it in the blood soaked pant leg, and bound it with the rope I had been tied with.

"I have to get you some help," I said. I left him for a minute and quickly made a travois out of two tree branches. Using the backpack my uniform shirt and pants, I managed to make a passable device that I could use to haul him. I quickly dressed in the orange robe of the monastery and started dragging.

I knew that we were near a village, since I had recognized our campsite the night before. It couldn't be any more than a mile from the stream where we camped.

I glanced back at the crater and spotted the AK-47, looking miraculously unscathed in the bottom of the crater. I thought briefly about climbing down and retrieving it, but figured the guy might die if I took any extra time. So I turned back towards the village and pulled on the poles.

I hadn't gone more than a few hundred yards when I came upon the backpack the monks had given me, the same one that my captor had taken from me. I stooped and found a canteen half full of water and took a long swig. I poured some of it down the throat of the unconscious man in the travois. Surprisingly, he seemed to be swallowing most of it. My leg was throbbing and seeping blood, but I knew that if there was any chance of saving this guy, I had better keep moving.

I pulled on the poles for hours, checking every so often by glancing back at the unconscious form on the travois. Each time, I could see the slight rise and fall of the chest. As long as he was breathing, I knew I wasn't just dragging a dead guy on some sticks. That would be fun to try to explain to a bunch of Viet Cong.

A slight movement somewhere off to my right caught my attention so I stopped. A few seconds later the head of a small boy appeared in the tall grass. He looked at me with that same impassive face of my former captor. It occurred to me that they learned to mask their feelings mighty young around here.

Shortly, he stood up. He was maybe eight or nine years old. He stared hard at my cargo, and finally approached.

He stood there on the trail, studying me for a while. He kept returning his gaze to my face, then my oozing foot, and then to the travois.

"Is he your friend," he asked softly. I understood the question perfectly, but considered for a time before answering.

"Yes, he saved my life,"

"Is he Republican?" the boy asked, all businesslike.

I shook my head, "No, Viet Cong." I did not like where this was going. "You are American." It was definitely not a question. I nodded. I wanted to explain that I had been badly wounded, nurtured back to life by Buddhist monks. But I doubted if he was interested in the details.

"Could we just get him some help? He is very close to dying," I asked. "This way," he motioned. He darted off to the right, up a slight hill and towards an outcropping rock.

It was not really a trail, but maybe it was a shortcut. It occurred to me that he could be leading me into an ambush, but he took off so fast I just hurried after him. He disappeared from sight so I called out, "Please go slower! My foot will not allow me to run."

He reappeared tugging the hand of a small woman. Her black hair was starting to show twinges of gray and her face was stern as she checked the monk's robes out in detail. Then she went to the travois and put her hand on the man's brow.

A sob arose in her throat, and she covered her mouth. She spun to face me now, and her eyes were wide with rage. Without making a sound she lunged with both hands reaching for my throat.

Instinctively I dropped the poles of the travois and tried to duck off to the side. The man on the stretcher thudded to the ground in a heap. The boy yelled something I was too busy to understand as I made the bad mistake of putting my full weight on my bad foot, and collapsed in a heap myself. The woman fell right on top of me, missing my throat but wrapping her hands around my head.

"What have you done to him? What happened to his foot?"

With some effort, I dislodged her and held her above me. She clawed the air like a feral cat. I shook her until she stopped writhing.

"Can we just get him into a bed? He will bleed to death unless we can stabilize his wound! I can explain everything after I know he is safe."

She seemed startled that I could speak her language, and startled that I should care about the man on the stretcher. She looked right through me before deciding that what I said made sense.

I guided her to the earth beside me and she stood up, straightening her black cotton clothes and her dignity. Then she was all business. "You take the poles, Bon Nghe!"

The boy grabbed them and lifted the travois. He was surprisingly strong for his size. Now the woman turned to me. "You follow behind us, but stay outside of my home!"

I nodded, got to my feet and fell in behind the travois. I started to realize how exhausted I was as I trailed the sorry procession through a clearing and up to a small hut.

When we reached the hut I helped them put the unconscious form onto a cot. As soon as he was on his back she shoved me outside. I looked around at a couple of other huts, and slid to the ground with my back against the wall, took a deep breath and fell asleep.

I woke once during the night to feel someone cover me with a blanket. My neck ached and my butt hurt from sitting on the hard earth, so I stretched out flat under the blanket and slept.

Chapter 7

I awakened with the bright sun streaming in my face and the pressure of my K-bar knife against my spine. My foot was throbbing and my belly was tender and sore. I wondered what I was doing here, and then remembered the freckle-faced man who used to be my captor. I wondered if he had made it through the night. Maybe he still was my captor.

I gingerly got to my feet and looked at the door of the hut, and then at path leading to the jungle. If I was ever going to get back to some friendlies, this was about as good an opportunity as I would get. I started towards the woods, surprised to see that no one was watching.

Each time I set my right foot down and then

quickly hobbled onto the stronger left one. The going was slow, and I paused at the edge of the jungle and closed my eyes, hoping to hear the voice of the Abbot tell me it was all right to seek my freedom. Nothing.

So I sighed and then turned again towards the east. I had gone maybe ten steps when I heard a horrible scream from the hut. I stopped in my tracks.

In my mind I thought I heard Truong's voice saying, "You know the drill." Did it seem like he was smiling or chuckling? I turned around and hobbled back to the hut and opened the door.

My captor was sitting up on the cot, and the old woman and the boy were trying to wrestle him back down. When he saw me, he stopped, and the woman and the boy turned to stare.

In English I said, "If you try to walk, you'll probably be dead in ten minutes. Lay back down."

He focused his eyes as if he was seeing a ghost. For a short moment he just stared, then he sighed, and lay back down.

I turned to the woman and the boy. I said in Vietnamese, "I need medicine…morphine ... A medical kit." The boy nodded and scooted out the door. The woman looked at me without saying a word. She picked up a damp rag and wiped the brow of the man on the cot.

Soon enough the boy reappeared with another man in black with an AK- 47 and a US Army field medical kit, the kind the Medics carried. He studied me for a minute but didn't offer the kit.

The boy said, "Auntie Mai. This is the same monk who brought uncle to me." The man frowned, and glanced at the woman. She nodded.

The soldier grunted. "If he dies, so do you," he said as he pushed the kit at me.

The boy looked at the man with the weapon and turned and left the hut. I wasn't sure whether I should take the medical kit or not. My captor was barely alive, and I wasn't trained as a medic. If I were a betting man, I'd put all my money on his dying.

"I am not sure I can save him," I said, "he's nearly dead now."

The man in black raised his weapon to the middle of my chest, and pushed the kit at me. "So are you."

I thought I'd try another tact. "He has lost a lot of blood, and I had to remove his foot yesterday to drag him here. I will do what I can." I took the kit and opened it. It was intact.

I found the morphine and handed it to the woman, "Please see that he drinks all of it," I asked. She nodded and took the yellow liquid.

I focused again on the leg. I had seen a battlefield amputation once when I first came to Nam. It was not pretty, and it was not a success. Two medics had worked for nearly an hour, and the kid died on the table the next day anyway.

Auntie Mai poured the pale fluid down my captor's throat, and he coughed twice and drifted off. "Keep at it until the bottle is empty." I said, "He will need it all."

She frowned but forced his mouth open and trickled more into him. I pulled back the blanket and surveyed the leg.

The pant-leg that I had used as a bandage was soaked with blood, and it had started to coagulate into the material. I asked the woman to get hot water and rags and did my best to clean it.

I found the needles and sutured the flap of skin snugly against the raw bone, washing it in iodine as I worked. I hoped to stop the loss of blood, and kill any infections, but had no clue as to whether it would work. Mostly I was just going through the motions, trying to mimic the medics I had seen.

I looked up once to check on the patient, and saw a face so pale that the freckles under his eyes stood out like brown ink dots on parchment paper. It occurred to me that I was trying to save the life of a Vet Cong soldier, and would probably be shot for treason for it. *"Oh well,* I thought, *"I would probably be shot today for sure if it all didn't work out."*

When I again focused on the leg, it looked hopeless. The guy looked like he was a goner. He had all the same signs as that kid I had seen the two medics try to save. With the same deathly white skin, shallow breathing and a high temperature I wondered how long until he gasped and died like the young soldier.

It occurred to me that I had better watch my thinking. The Abbot used to tell us not to expect anything, but not to be surprised either. The man with the gun stood passively by, watching my every move.

Sweat was starting to show on the ashen face of my patient, so I grabbed a wet rag and wiped his forehead. Just then the door opened and three more men in black pajamas walked in. Each had his weapon in his hand.

"I need more medical supplies," I said to the closest one. "I am out of morphine and almost out of Iodine, and I need more thread for the sutures."

Four weapons came up, each aimed at my face or chest. Four sets of eyes focused intently on my face. The oldest one spoke, "Who are you?"

I paused with the stitching, and studied their faces. I guess all Vietnamese are taught to mask all of their emotions as a rite of passage.

I sighed. "I am a Buddhist monk." For some strange reason it sounded almost like the truth. Maybe it was. For a tense moment the weapons remained pointed at my chest. One by one they lowered them. A quick nod from the one who obviously was in command, and a young soldier opened the door and left.

More medical supplies appeared within minutes. I took them and bowed to the soldier when he handed the package to me. Surprisingly, he returned the bow.

I did what I could for the man, and as I worked I thought of the Abbot. He had lectured on the idea that our work was to be continuously in the moment. Each moment was to be the entire focus of our effort, our total concentration. I nodded to myself and tried to be totally the medic.

I focused on the sutures. I forced myself to let go of any thought that was not about sutures, not about the now. I made myself stay in the present, watching each time the needle entered the skin and exited at the other side. I watched the black thread to make sure it didn't catch or knot or anything. I constantly patted the area around the sutures with a clean cloth, daubing up the seeping blood.

At one point I grabbed a bucket and thrust it into the face of one of the soldiers. "Hot water. Now."

He nodded and glanced at the older one, who nodded also. Within ten minutes he returned with some hot water. I took it and bowed slightly and thanked him. Without a pause, he returned the bow.

I finished up and washed the blood off my hands in the last of the cooling water. I surveyed my handiwork, and didn't see any signs of seeping blood. I hoped I had remembered all the steps.

The oldest of the soldiers watched me impassively. After I had washed and checked the wound he spoke. "Who are you, long nose?"

The barrel of his AK-47 moved again to a position just inches from my nose. "Long-nose" is an insulting way of describing someone who is not from Asia.

"I am a Buddhist monk. I received my training at the Golden Lotus Monastery by Abbot Ngyuen. Before I was a monk I was an American soldier."

The man turned to the boy, who was standing near the woman. "Bon Nghel, go and find those monks that were near the rice paddies. Bring them here. Now!"

The boy darted out the door, leaving me with my captor, Auntie Mai, and four Viet Cong soldiers. Suddenly this hut seemed way too small.

"May I sit?" I asked as I nearly fell to the floor. I was totally exhausted. The man in charge nodded. "You may as well sit, you are not going anywhere."

I sat on the floor, crossed my legs into the lotus pose and closed my eyes. I thought I would demonstrate how well trained I was as a monk, but I just fell asleep sitting there.

The smell of food woke me up. I opened my eyes to see that darkness was coming. I tried to remember my last meal, but couldn't think of it at all. The woman had tidied up the place, and the four men were sitting with their backs against the wall. All were eating from small white bowls.

The woman noticed that I was awake and handed me a bowl of fish and rice. I thanked her automatically and closed my eyes to offer a silent blessing on the food. While my eyes were closed, she snatched the bowl away. I opened my eyes to see what happened.

"I am so sorry," she said. "I have forgotten my manners. I know monks are not going to eat meat or fish. Please forgive me."

"I took no offense, and so there is nothing to forgive," I said.

She quickly removed the fish and handed the bowl back to me. I didn't tell her that I probably would have eaten the fish without thinking, even though Buddhist monks are all vegetarians. I bowed to her and silently thanked her for probably saving my life.

I could taste the rice that had contacted the fish, and it sure seemed to taste good. I remembered that suffering comes from wanting, and so I decided I didn't really want any fish. I pushed that thought of fish out of my mind and focused on the rice and the vegetables, remembering to be grateful for the food. I ate slowly as I had been taught to do. I savored each bite and focused entirely on the act of eating. As a result, everyone else finished eating long before I did.

After the meal I got to my feet and checked on the patient. The four men watched impassively. His fever had gone down and maybe his color was coming back a little. His breathing was shallow little gasps, but at least it was regular. The wound and the sutures looked okay. At least there was no seeping blood or swelling.

The door opened and a man and a boy entered. They bowed and sat against the back wall, scooting close beside the four soldiers. No sooner were they seated than the door opened again and a farmer and his wife and a very old woman, probably the farmer's mother came in. They too bowed and sat.

This hut seemed way too small for so many people, and I thought I might want to step outside and give them more room, since it looked like a village meeting was about to take place.

Auntie Mai stood up and produced three candles from some fold in her clothing, and a match and three tiny plates. She lit the candles, dripping some wax onto each plate and then set the candles in the cooling wax.

She turned to me and said, "Brother Monk, where would you like these placed?"

"Oh God! I thought. *"All these folks are here for instructions!"* I bowed and tried to mask my surprise, and waived my hand in the direction of a large wooden crate that stood on its side. Auntie Mai reverently placed the candles on the crate, backed away and bowed and sat down.

I wished I had told them that I was just an acolyte, a monk in training. I sure as hell never meant to imply I was an elder. But I just followed the same routine I had seen so many rainy days in the monastery, except instead of sitting at the edge of the circle, I sat in the center.

First there is a long silent prayer, then the leader (in this case me) calls on the spirit of Buddha, the Compassionate One, and all the Bodhisattvas (that'd be all the awakened masters) to be present and speak through my voice to impart wisdom. Noble Truths?"

I nodded and bowed slightly. In certain sects the most senior layman would offer a question, and the monk would direct his discourse to the question asked. I had been told that while this was often true, when a revered monk was present, the group would defer to him by letting him choose the discussion topic.

I wondered if the old man was testing me, or simply following his tradition. Either way, it would probably not have been a good idea to upset a man with so much authority, and a loaded gun.

So I half closed my eyes the same way the Abbot did when he was about to begin a lecture. If a lecture was wanted, I would give it to them.

The Abbot often said that the best way to learn something is to teach it, and this looked like a great time to start. I began with the opening words of the lecture I had heard at least ten times; the one called the Four Noble Truths.

"All life is suffering. This is the first Noble Truth." I looked around to see how it was going, and remembered what the Abbot had said that first time, "When we teach, we try to give examples that apply to those listening"

I waived my hand around the room. "Here in this house we see that suffering. This crazy war shows us our suffering." The older man's face went dark, and he scowled.

"It is not just my suffering," I continued. "Nor is it just your suffering. We all suffer. All sentient beings suffer. It is the way of things. But the Second Noble Truth tells us that suffering can be alleviated." I was really warming up to it now. Trying to imitate the old Abbot in all his mannerisms.

"Suffering can be alleviated by giving up wanting and not wanting. Because what we desire and what we abhor is what causes our suffering. It is not the event that brings the suffering. No! Not the event, but our thoughts about the event that brings the suffering!"

I watched their faces, trying in vain to read them. "That," I said dramatically, "is the third Noble Truth."

Nothing in their faces let me know if I was making any sense to them so I pressed on. "The foreigners, like me, we all want to go home. But we are not at home, and so we suffer! The people of Viet Nam want the foreigners gone, and they are not all gone, and so they suffer."

"The politicians suffer because they want things that they don't have, or they have things that they don't want." I still had no clue as to whether I was making any sense. I decided that I should just let the Abbot speak through me. It didn't take long before I was listening to myself as if I were sitting in the audience hearing the old Abbot.

Often as I talked, I noticed the door of the hut came open and another person would enter. The hut was tiny to begin with, and the man on the cot took up a large portion, but through the evening it turned into standing room only.

I looked up once to see the door open again. This time, two young monks bowed and entered. The crowd parted and they made their way up to the small patch of open floor right in front of me, where they bowed again and sat down, looking directly at me.

I panicked! I had no idea what I was going to say! I was sure they would expose me as a fraud! My mind went blank.

I closed my eyes, remembering Truong and his great stalling tactic when I would ask him a question. Immediately I heard his soft voice within myself.

"Toby," he said. "You are just fine."

I certainly didn't feel just fine, and I still had no clue what to say next! "Get yourself out of the way, just as you were taught. Let truth speak through you.   Remember when you quoted from your small book that beautiful saying? Remember it now, and stand back!"

I barely remembered that discussion, but I did remember that I thumbed furiously through the book until I found that quote from the Book of Matthew.

" By myself I can do nothing. It is not I, but the Father within, who doeth the work."

And so I imagined myself sitting aside, and letting the Father Within continue the lecture. I was a little concerned about whether the Father Within had ever heard of the Buddhist teachings, but by myself I was sure I couldn't come up with any better plan. Somehow, the evening passed.

There was not a sense of trying to think or remember or put it in any order. I guess I just let it fly, and it must have made some impression. It was only when I heard myself pause and look around to a silent room that I remembered that no one was going to leave unless I excused them.

I wanted to excuse them, and like so many of them more than once I had sat on my butt on a hard floor and wished the lecture would end and he would excuse us. But he never did. First there had to be a long silent meditation.

I closed my eyes, thinking tonight I might just make a change, and have a short meditation, but the Truong's voice seemed to whisper conspiratorially inside of me.

It said, "Show them how to meditate, Toby!"

So I cleared my mind and began to notice my breathing. It wasn't long before I found the "sweet spot." It is a place in between thoughts, where the room seems to flood with light, even though the eyes remains shut.

Nearly an hour past before I heard some fidgeting and coughing. I reluctantly left the meditation and opened my eyes. Like the Abbot had taught me, I clapped my hands loudly, bringing everyone's attention back.

I struggled to my feet and bowed. Every person in the room except the man on the cot stood immediately and bowed back to me as one. Then each person came up to me and bowed and thanked me. I folded my hands and blessed each one.

The tiny hut began to empty. I had forgotten the two monks until they stood in front of me. Each one clasped his hands and bowed deeply, almost to the waist. I blessed them with a bow, and they filtered out the door, until only the woman, the boy and the old soldier remained. I was very tired, and wondered if and when I could sleep.

"You are a good teacher," she said, "but a very strange monk. Would you care for some tea?"

Since it is a huge insult to refuse tea, I bowed and said that I would love some. I sat back down in silence and watched as she began heating the tea water in a white porcelain pot with an old fashioned whistling top.

"Auntie Mai," the boy shouted. "Uncle Bien has opened his eyes!"

I surprised myself by getting to my feet so quickly, and was nearly the first one to the cot. Auntie Mai placed her hand on Bien's forehead and gently massaged it. "The heat is nearly gone," she said softly.

I checked the wound, and it all looked okay, and noticed that his breathing was deep and regular. He studied me intently as I checked his pulse and verified that his temperature had receded.

"You had your chance to go. Why did you not leave me?" His voice was surprisingly strong for someone I thought wouldn't live until morning.

I pondered the question, since I had asked the very same one to myself. Finally I said, "It didn't seem like the thing to do at the time."

A brief flicker danced across his face, to be quickly supplanted by his poker face. Then his eyes closed and he slept.

The whistle of the teapot started to go, and Auntie Mai quickly was at the stove, removing the pot. The boy and I stood by the cot for a moment, watching his rhythmic breathing.

In Vietnamese the boy said, "He got luck. He had a good doctor."

When the tea had been seeped and the boy had gone out the door, Auntie Mai brought the steaming cup to me. She bowed and backed away.

"Aren't you having some too?" I asked. She turned and poured another cup and came and sat on the floor.

"Those monks were told to report that you are an imposter, but they would not do so. Did you know them?"

I shook my head. "Will they not be punished for disobeying?"

She studied me for a moment. "The soldier who sent for them was not so sure you are an imposter either. He respected the judgment of the monks. How long were you in the monastery?"

"I don't know," I said honestly. "Seven or eight months. Long enough to see parts of both monsoons. I was raised a Christian, and we had many great discussions."

She nodded intently, and asked," So are you a Christian or a Buddhist?"

I frowned. It was a good question, and I was not sure I had an answer.

"My Beloved Abbot," I said, surprised that I would speak of him using the title that Truong always used. "My beloved Abbot used to say that sometimes it's better to live in the question than find the answer."

She took that in but didn't ask anything else. I sipped the tea and concentrated on its flavor, and the warming sensation as it made its way down my throat.

"I see that you are injured too," she said finally. I nodded. "I was near death when the monks found me impaled in a tree. They took me down and nursed me back to health. Without them, I would have died."

She set down her cup, with most of the tea still in the cup. "Death seems to be everywhere. My husband and two sons are gone. I was sure I had lost my brother until you dragged him home."

We sat in silence, each sorting out the thoughts. I noticed again how tired I was. I had no idea if I would be tied up and locked in some hut, or left to sleep outside the door. She must have sensed my thinking.

"I am so sorry. I must get you a blanket. We can talk more in the morning, but I am tired and I can see you are also."

She went to a footlocker and produced a woolen blanket. I couldn't help but notice it had lettering on a small white label that said; "Property of the USMC."

I lay down at the foot of the cot and she covered me with the blanket. "Thank you for your kindness," I said. I was fading fast.

She was dousing the candles, making the room darker as she moved from candle to candle. But her voice was clear. "And you for yours," she said as the room went dark. I was asleep in less than a minute.

Chapter 8

Three young men, probably in their early teens, opened the door carrying their AK-47s in a ready position. Each wore the khaki uniform of the North Vietnamese Army, and each wearing the pith helmet so much favored by Uncle Ho. They quickly surveyed the room, pausing for a moment when they saw me sitting in my orange robe with my legs in the full lotus position.

One came right up to me and ordered me to stand up, which I did. He patted me down for a weapon and nodded to his comrade. His comrade opened the door and left.

Within a minute the door opened and the soldier returned with an older man who was tall and muscular and had just a hint of gray in his black hair. He carried himself with an air of command that made everyone take notice. He wore the plain black pajama look of Viet Cong, but his bearing was that of high-ranking officer.

I remembered a guy in my unit who could spot an officer no matter what he wore. I was told that they are drilled with the idea of a "command presence." This guy had that. His eyes quickly swept the hut. For some reason he reminded me of a panther. He moved with a lot of grace, but an implied power that would not tolerate any insubordination. The young soldiers treated him with utmost respect, and he made a point to acknowledge each person with eye contact and a bow. At last his eyes landed on me.

I bowed out of instinct, and he returned the bow, but only slightly. In flawless English he said, "May I know your name?"

Hearing English startled me. I guess maybe that was his tactic so I purposefully took some time before answering. My dad used to tell me that if you always tell the truth you don't need a good memory. That idea seemed to apply to the situation, so I bowed deeply again and said in Vietnamese, "My name is Toby Allman, how may I serve you?"

He got about halfway through another bow before he caught himself. It was his turn to be surprised, but he quickly masked it. "How long have you been in my country?" He could have said Viet Nam, or our country, but he made it real personal, "My country."

I took a deep breath, just like the Abbot taught. We were told to ask within before responding to any question. That way we would speak from our highest truth, and be led towards peace and union with our brother.

"I am not sure," I said formally. "I was near the last week of my tour when I was badly wounded. I was taken to a monastery and nursed back to health. I remained there a very long time and I now have no idea what month or even what year it is."

He studied me for some time. I had the vague feeling I was in a high stakes poker game, and he was trying to guess my hand.

"In the western calendar this would be March 13th, 1973." Again it was in perfect English.

He had nailed me on that one. I probably lost the game, the car and the mortgage. I had no idea so much time had passed. "My last patrol was the 19th of January, 1972." I said. That meant that I had been gone for some fourteen months. Inside my head I heard the old Abbot's gentle voice remind me that the truth is always appropriate.

"I had no idea how much time had passed," I said softly in English. "May I know your name?"

He stared at me for a long time. Maybe he was so important that everyone was supposed to know his name. Maybe he didn't want it known. I was reasonably certain that I had caught him off guard, though.

He bowed and announced, "I am Quang Liem. Did you not also know that most all the American Forces are gone, and the last of the advisors are leaving even as we speak?"

I nodded. I really didn't know it, but I strongly suspected that it he knew more about American troop movements than I did.

Auntie Mai bowed politely, apologized for interrupting, and invited us both to sit for tea. It was already made and steaming in two cups. My foot had been paining me ever since I had jumped to my feet when the boy soldiers pointed their weapons at me. I don't know if Auntie Mai had noticed it, but if she did, I was sure grateful.

Quang Liem bowed and said, "Yes, of course. Please forgive my rudeness. I was summoned here because there was a report of an American soldier in the village. Would you care to tell me which unit you were with?"

I froze. We were drilled with the idea that we were to give only our name, our rank, and our serial number. We were also warned that any other information we supplied would probably be construed as aiding and abetting the enemy.

He apparently saw my dilemma. "You may have been part of the 101st Airborne Division. The last of those soldiers left headquarters on the last day

January, 1972."

Since he had correctly guessed my unit, and he knew when I was supposed to leave, I wondered if it still mattered. So I simply nodded.

As he accepted his tea and sat at the low table he added, "I am the District Provost. I had to see this American soldier for myself."

I carefully sat on the floor and Auntie Mai placed my teacup and saucer before me. Next she produced tea for the three young soldiers, and a cup for herself. We all sat in silence at the table.

The Abbot's conspiratorial voice whispered to me to remember to say a blessing. I quickly closed my eyes and waited the appropriate time before asking the spirit of the Lord Buddha's loving-kindness to be the host.

After the blessing, Quang Liem turned to me. In English he said, "So tell me about your time in the temple."

I wasn't sure whether he was trying to impress me with his language skills or if he didn't want the others to find out what was being said. But after my encounters on the trail, I had decided it was best to answer in the language that the question is asked. But it felt strange to be speaking English again.

"The monks said I died and came back. I was really badly wounded, and I found out later that there was speculation about how many days I would live. They told me that it was a good omen that I had died and come back." He nodded and sipped the tea, studying the leaves.

"How did you pass the time at the monastery?"

"We talked." I said simply.

He placed the cup carefully into the saucer and turned and looked directly at me. He smiled, but there was no warmth in the smile. "What, exactly, did you talk about?"

The change in his voice, and the change in his tone set off an alarm in my brain. This was starting to sound like an interrogation. And I might just accidentally say the wrong thing and end up as the target of a firing squad. Suddenly I was very nervous.

I cleared my throat, stalling for time, hoping to get some inspiration as to what to say. The silence was deafening.

I opened my mouth, figuring that somehow something would occur to me, but there was nothing, so I closed it. He continued to look right though me. My mind was racing with various stories that might somehow keep me out of trouble, but each one sounded more dangerous than the last. Finally I heard the Abbot's voice. "Always tell the truth, Brother Toby."

So I did just that. I told him of the firefight, and the death of my team. I didn't exactly go into detail about the part about the losses for his side.

But I told him of the monks finding me, and the rainy seasons in the temple, and my learning the language, and the long discussions about Buddha.

I told him how patient the monks were when I had the fevers and the chills, and how they poured tea down me. I even told him of my desire to sneak away and find my way back to America.

He smiled when I told him about the gifts from all the monks and how they "allowed" me to escape.

But then his eyes turned cold, and he said, "So, you were trying to get back to your unit, or to any U.S. unit?"

I knew that if I answered that question, I would probably be shot. Even to my mind, it sure sounded like admitting to being an enemy combatant, sneaking around in a country where I didn't belong.

I thought about Bien, and finding him so badly wounded, and sawing through his ankle-bone. I was so glad I hadn't taken his weapon with me when I dragged him to the village,

But they might still see me as a spy dressed as a monk. For the life of me I couldn't think of anything to say in answer to that question.

A weak voice from the darkened part of the hut said, "Why would an American soldier take the time and effort to save his captor, and then drag him all the way to a hostile village?"

I turned and glanced at the man on the cot. I had completely forgotten that he spoke English. In fact I had nearly forgotten he was in the room.

Quang Liem was staring at him too.

Now he turned back to me. "Why, indeed," he said softly.

"I really can't answer that question." I mumbled.

From somewhere inside my brain, I was sure I could hear the high-pitched giggle of Truong, and a quote from his Beloved Abbot too, Truong's silent voice inside me said, "The path to knowing comes through the land of not-knowing."

Quang Liem studied me for a long moment. His hands were clasped together on the low table, and I saw his thumbs begin to slowly tap together. For some time those thumbs were the only movement in the room. It was so quiet that I actually heard the soft thud when the two thumbs contacted each other.

Finally he stood up and approached Bien's cot. He placed his hand on Bien's forehead, and left it there for a while. It reminded me of a father or grandfather taking the temperature of a beloved family member.

Then he turned to me.

"Perhaps, sir, you are just finding out who you really are."

With that he bowed and strode to the door. His three young companions jumped quickly to their feet, grabbed their weapons and followed him out.

Mai busied herself clearing up the china. Our eyes met briefly and I thought maybe I detected a smile, but she turned away before I could be sure.

With her back to me she said in a firm voice, "It's getting late in the afternoon. I might suggest that you decide what tonight's lecture should be about."

I realized I had been holding my breath for some time, so I slowly exhaled and bowed. It occurred to me that right mindfulness would be the perfect thing to talk about tonight. Once again I swear I heard Truong's voice giggle.

So I spoke that evening on Right Mindfulness. I imitated the old Abbot, and was amazed that I could nearly recall word for word his entire lecture right down to his dramatic pauses, and his stories to illustrate each point.

About halfway through the lecture the room got so full that the village elder suggested we move to the largest building in the village. By the time we all got relocated and the talk was finished, and the long and silent meditation was over, it was nearly midnight.

I spoke every night after that, but tried to cut down the time a little. The crowds kept growing, and many people came from nearby villages. Soon enough the village elders decided to locate us in the nearby Province of Lam Dong, just across the river. There was an abandoned Catholic church, and it was plenty big enough.

I don't know how many days passed in Lam Dong, but the monsoons came and went, and still I lectured, discussing the Suttras, and occasionally counseling a couple or performing a funeral or a marriage.

A young man appeared one day at the door to the temple and informed me that he wanted to follow the path of the Lord Buddha. I bowed and invited him to sit for ten lectures. I told him that after ten lectures he would know if this was his path.

He nodded and bowed and said, "I am Phuoc. I am sure that this is my path, but I will obey your wish and sit for ten lectures. Is there a place where I can sleep?"

I showed him our four cots. Since only mine was being used, he took the one on the other side of the room.

"Brother Phuoc, you are welcome to stay as long as you would like. Would you be offended if I called you Honored sir?"

He bowed again and said, "From this day forward my name is Honored Sir. I am grateful for your kindness."

And so our little temple now had two monks. Honored Sir quickly adapted to the rituals and patterns of the temple. Each morning I would school him much the way Beloved Abbot had schooled me. Like me, he asked a lot of questions, and like the Abbot, I tried to be as clear as I could in the answers. I found it helped me to clarify my own understanding to explain it to him.

Occasionally, I would hear news of the war. It

seemed that the Americans had left in a big hurry, and the Southern forces had lost their will. Desertions from the Southern forces were massive, and only small pockets of resistance were being encountered. Many soldiers from the south who wouldn't desert were being executed. The northern forces were not prepared for the rapid disintegration of the ARVN armies, and couldn't advance fast enough to take the places the south had abandoned.

One night, in the middle of our meditation and chanting, I heard the door open and close. I was facing away from the door, and assumed it was a farmer who had decided I was too long-winded.

After the service ended, I was cleaning up and straightening the altar when a voice behind me said, "Brother Toby!" I turned quickly, surprised that I was not alone. Honored Sir had asked for leave to attend the funeral of his grandmother, and wasn't expected back for another week.

I collided with a monk in an orange robe. I blinked in the dim light to see who it was. I recognized the voice before I did the image. Troung's voice was weaker than I remembered.

'Toby Allman, That was a wonderful lecture tonight!"

"Brother Truong I" I shouted. I grabbed him and lifted him off the ground, and spun around, nearly tripping. He was thinner than I remembered, and didn't seem as healthy.

Ordinarily physical contact between monks is most unusual. In fact, the entire society seemed to have an aversion to physical contact except for the women in a family hugging each other. It might have been inappropriate, but I had to admit I was mighty glad to see him. His face was bright red, and his smile was nearly ear to ear.

"How did you find me?" I asked as I started a fire and put on water for tea.

His face got serious. "We had quite a visit from some gentlemen from the provisional government," Truong explained. "At first we thought they were coming there to close our temple, but they assured us that they only wanted to know about an American monk."

He looked around suspiciously, "They asked so many questions about you. You may be in great danger!"

I was surprised. I knew that they watched my every move, and made daily reports about me. But I passed that off as normal paranoia that seemed to be a part of their culture. They had rules about everyone becoming the eyes for the party.

"But I thought everything was good," I said. "No soldiers have come to bother me in a long while."

Truong lowered his eyes. "The war is almost over. Now the factional fighting begins. There are hardliners, and there are moderates. No one has any idea which group will prevail."

"Hardliners?" I asked. He nodded. "Hardliners

want to destroy all religions and create a Marxist state. And they want to purge the party of any moderates. The moderates want Viet Nam to return to a place where Buddhism is the religion, and the people are free to do the will of the party."

The tea water boiled, and I served my honored friend. He went on to explain that certain elements wanted to reconcile with the ARVN troops and other groups wanted to execute them all. Viet Nam was becoming a very dangerous place.

"I thought that the war was about getting rid of foreigners," I said.

Truong shook his head. "It is much more complicated than that. The north is driven and funded by money from China and Russia. Both have embraced the ideology of communism, which has a goal to rid the world of religions."

He frowned, with wrinkles magically appearing on his smooth face. "There was a common enemy, which is disintegrating, and now the factions will struggle for power."

I sipped my tea, thinking about the fact that I had managed to convince myself that I might make a home for myself. It was almost as if I was willing myself to forget that my goal was to escape. The Abbot had lectured about the life of a monk, often repeating that a monk is to avoid getting attached to anyone or anything or any place.

Truong broke into my reverie, "The north is winning the war, but there will be a struggle to win the peace. You must go now to Saigon, before it falls."

"Saigon? Why Saigon?"

Truong leaned close to me and whispered, "There is an American embassy still in Saigon. When it falls, the purges will begin."

"Purges?"

He nodded. "They will round up anyone that has been accused of conspiring with the South. They may execute anyone who is religious. Or they may let the religions be."

He put his hand on my arm, and leaned close. His face showed tiredness I had never seen before. "You may be sure that an American who used to be a soldier will not have many friends to protect him."

"What about the Abbot?" I asked. "Maybe he is in danger too." Truong lowered his eyes. "That is the other thing I came here to tell you. The Abbot is not well. He has asked about you."

"Me? Why would he ask about me?"

A big smile appeared on Troung's face. "He said to tell you that he misses your profound questions."

It was my turn to smile, "Yeah, right!" I said.

Instantly Truong's face lost its smile. His eyes suddenly focused on the floor. "Do you remember what he told us about telling the truth? I would not tease about that."

"I'm sorry," I said. "I meant no slight. I just find it hard to think that he would ever bother to think of me."

Truong looked right into my eyes. "He said to tell you that he only speaks to you when you summon him. He said you probably saved your life by telling the official the truth. And he said that you would know what that meant."

My mouth dropped open and my mind seemed to race and screech to a halt and race again. If he could really be inside my head and talk to me, then my view of the world was seriously flawed. I was suddenly exhausted.

"I am out of energy," I finally managed to say. "You can make your bed in one of those cots. But I really have to sleep, and soon."

I stood and bowed, and so did he. I showed him where the cots were and went to my own.

That night, I dreamed of explosions and fire and loud screams. I saw the sights and heard the sounds, and yet somehow remained just outside the dream. As I slept, I found my mind remembering a vivid discussion with a blob of bright light. But I couldn't quite recall the contents of that discussion.

At breakfast Truong told me that the Abbot was insisting that the temple be moved to Laos. The ruler of Laos had assured both the Buddhists and the Catholics that they would be free to practice their beliefs without interference from the government. With the situation becoming so uncertain in Viet Nam, the Abbot wished to avoid any difficulties.

"And so, Brother Toby, the monastery where you

had spent so much time has been abandoned."

Truong showed me a map, with distances to Saigon. He even marked on it safe places to camp for the nights. "You must go immediately. There is no telling how long before the South Vietnamese government falls. And when it does, the Americans will be gone."

"We must be near Laos right here. If the Abbot is not well, I will to go with you to see him."

He shook his head. "No! You must leave for Saigon! Toby, an acquaintance of mine made some discreet inquiries, and you are not considered a traitor. You are officially listed as "missing in action, presumed dead."

"I would never leave Viet Nam without saying goodbye to Beloved Abbot."

I stood up and made up a quick tote bag that contained my bowl, a small teapot with four tiny cups, and a second pair of tire-sole sandals. Truong watched me in silence as I gathered some food. "Will three days food be enough?" I asked.

He nodded, stood up and sighed. "You Americans are sure hard headed," he muttered.

The door to the temple opened and closed. Truong looked at me and I looked at him. Just then I heard the voice of Honored Sir. "Master Toby, I have returned! My grandmother was quite alive! Someone had made a big mistake when they sent word she had died."

Truong looked at me with a big smile, "You are now Master Toby!" He bowed deeply and with a lot of flourish. "I am so honored to hear of your promotion."

I opened my mouth to explain about Honored Sir, and how he showed up one day, but before I could say anything, Honored Sir was in the room. He saw Truong, and bowed deeply.

Now Troung returned the bow, and I had to do the whole introduction thing. Honored Sir was so pleased to meet Truong, and began immediately asking about the time at the temple.

Truong managed to catch my eye and rolled his as the young man continued to rapidly ask questions. I smiled and finished packing.

After about twenty minutes of non-stop talking and asking questions I felt sorry enough for Truong that I interrupted them, I could see the relief on Truong's face.

" Honored Sir, I am so glad you are here. Brother Truong has come to tell me my honored Abbot has summoned me. I must go immediately and may be gone for a couple of weeks."

The look on his face was one of disbelief. Honored Sir was not about to tell me that I was under constant observation, and that he was the main informer. So I made it easy for him.

"Oh, and would you please get word to Mr. Quang Liem and send him my apologies for such a hasty departure. Each moment I stay may mean that my Beloved Abbot grows weaker."

I stepped past Honored Sir in the doorway, with Truong right on my tail. Outside, we both turned and bowed deeply to the flustered young monk before walking briskly out of the village and to the west.

Chapter 9

We walked westward in silence. It seemed like it was mostly downhill, which made it easier for me with my foot still giving me occasional pain. Truong's only comment was that I seemed much healthier than the last time he had seen me. I was not much in the mood for conversation, and glad that he seemed to sense that. And so the hours and the miles passed.

We made good time, and I was pleased to find my foot was stronger. It was not even sore until late in the day. We camped overnight near a Catholic church, and were back walking before the sun could be seen.

At lunch Truong told me that he had made some discreet inquiries through his brother, and found that I was listed as Missing in Action, presumed dead. "If you get to Saigon, you will be able to return to America. There will most likely not be any trouble, since your unit pulled out while you were wounded."

I began to think about going home. I was surprised to find that I had very mixed feelings about it. I didn't even know if my dad was still alive, and I had no idea where I would go or what I would do when I got back.

My last letter from my mother had said that dad's health was failing, and that had been months before my last mission. Now as we walked, Truong talked more and more, and I grew quieter and quieter.

Truong did tell me that the little cook who had found my bible and kept it for me had died when he stepped on a landmine. And he told me that the Abbot's heart was failing, and there was concern that he might die during the rigorous trip to Laos. Not exactly the kind of news that would cheer someone up.

We passed the many miles almost without noticing, and before long we stood on the shore of the Mekong River, the border between Viet Nam and Laos.

The landscape had changed from mountainous to flat, and from thick forest to thicker jungle. And it had grown warmer as we descended the mountains. Now that we stood in silence looking across the river it was oppressively hot. Sweat filled my eyes and the sting of salt didn't exactly improve my mood.

I guess I was waiting for Truong to speak, and he was waiting for me. I looked around, and saw NVA troops everywhere. It felt so strange to see them and not panic or feel threatened. But why would they fear a couple of Buddhist monks with nothing but begging bowls and a backpack?

I couldn't believe how much the area had changed. I had conducted patrols in this area when I first got to Viet Nam. At that time American troops were everywhere. The villagers used to play host to Americans during the day, and the Viet Cong at night.

Now the North Vietnamese Army was everywhere. Most of the soldiers were laughing and celebrating the collapse of the ARVN forces. Soldiers in any army are alike in many ways. Most of their time is spent waiting, and to wait is to talk, to brag and to regale their fellow soldiers. And soldiers in almost every army are experts on appearing busy while wasting time. I watched them with some amusement until the voice of the Abbot appeared in my head. "We are much more alike than we are different, are we not?"

The sight of two monks hardly even caught the attention of anyone, even when Truong left me alone while he arranged passage on a ferryboat across the river. I was not even given a second glance as we crowded onto an ancient boat with an old gasoline engine that ran at about three hundred RPM. It sounded like it was about to throw a rod, and didn't have the energy or the power to make it across the river. But it did. And the ride only took about ten minutes.

There was no customs officer in Laos, and so we simply walked off the boat and out of the village. Our new temple was supposedly only four miles into Laos. After at least five or six miles I began to suspect that Truong might be lost.

"Have you been here before?" I asked while he pondered a fork in the road.

"No." He said, looking up and down the road. He looked again in both directions, apparently looking for some landmark that was not there. Finally he suggested we make a late lunch.

We were sitting beside the path sipping tea when an old farmer appeared leading a water buffalo. He approached us and bowed, so we stood up and bowed back. After we gave him tea and some manioc, Truong spoke, "We are on our way to a temple, but don't seem to know its direction. I was told it was right on the path, but no one mentioned a fork."

The old man nodded. His eyes studied me for a long time. "Are you American?" he asked warily.

"I was born in America. Now I am a Buddhist monk," I answered.

He digested that, and lit a cigarette, which he

smoked right down to his fingers. If he was going to tell us about the temple, he was taking his sweet time. When I was sure he would burn his fingers and his mouth, he suddenly stood and tossed his cigarette stub on the ground. He ground it out with the heel of his sandal.

"Follow me," he said.

I glanced at Truong, who simply shrugged. So we followed him to untie his buffalo, and then we followed him back the way he had come.

The thought occurred to me that he might be leading us to an army unit, or a rural police station, but Truong seemed intent on just following him so I tagged along.

After nearly two hours or so of steadily climbing, he coaxed the buffalo to the side of the path and tied him to a tree. He motioned with his hand, and we followed through the forest cover.

He was totally off of any path, and we scrambled up a steep hill using our hands to steady ourselves and pull us forward. At the top of the hill he stopped.

Truong and I looked around, but saw nothing. I was about to speak when Truong said, "Pardon me, kind sir, but I don't see anything."

He pointed off in the distance at another hill. I was sure he was trying to pull a fast one.

"Aha, I see it!" Truong called. I looked again, but saw nothing.

The old farmer smiled. "The new Pathet Lao

government officially does not approve of religions, so many make themselves hard to see."

He smiled at us and bowed, and then made the sign of the cross. We thanked him and waived goodbye as he left. We waited until he was out of sight before we started down the hill towards an outcropping of rocks that blended into the landscape. Only an opening in the rock that was really a window suggested the presence of humans.

Before we had crossed the meadow and started up the hill the sound of a conch horn announced our arrival. A feeling of homesickness overcame me as the faces of monks began to appear, each one waiving to us. We entered through a small wooden door near the back of the large rock.

Monks began to appear everywhere. There were many more here than I could recall having seen in Viet Nam. There was even a cluster of nuns, drawn by the commotion.

We were tired and hungry by the time we had climbed the hill, but all that went away with the news that the Abbot was eager to see us.

The old doctor who attended to my wounds when I was bedridden greeted us warmly. " Brother Truong and Brother Toby, please follow me. We have a meal being prepared, and you may wish to see the Beloved Abbot right after dinner."

We bathed and ate quickly, and soon enough we were led to the chamber where the Abbot lay. I was shocked to see how tiny he was. He must have lost a lot of weight with his illness. But although his body was wasted, his eyes were as bright as ever. He tried to sit up to greet us, but the old doctor firmly pushed him back.

I bowed deeply, as did Truong. He held his arms out and we approached him from each side. He looked like he had aged fifty years since I had last seen him. It was sort of like he had held time at arm's length for a long time, and when he turned away for a moment it had rushed him and captured him.

He smiled. "Brother Toby, you surely recall the words from your small black book?"

I was numb with shock, and trying to hold back the tears. I shook my head. I had no idea what he was talking about.

He giggled, and in the dim lit room I recognized that cosmic giggle that had been with me since I had left the monastery.

"My younger brother returns," he said. "And he has forgotten what he taught this old man."

I looked at Truong, hoping he knew what the Abbot was talking about. He shrugged.

"Didn't you read to me from your book once? Didn't you say that the great teacher of the westerners taught that we were to "judge not by appearances?"

"Brothers Truong and Toby, don't be so glum! You are sad because you think I am leaving. Where could I go?" His voice seemed like it was stronger now.

Truong wiped a tear from his eye and said, "You don't have to go. You could just stay for a while longer."

The old man squeezed my hand and Truong's. "Come here" he said. We both leaned closer. His breath was light and stale, and his face was white.

"I watched you both grow and blossom like tender lotus flowers. You have blessed this old man with your humor, and your curiosity, and..." he turned to me, "your profound questions."

I was trying to calm myself, "What will happen to us? To the temple? Who will lead us when you...when you are not here?"

A huge smile lit up his face, and a sense of peacefulness seemed to fill him with color and beauty. He chuckled again, "You already know the answer to that question, Brother Toby. You have a companion within you, and you are learning to call on Him. What need have you of an outside teacher when you have apprehended your inner one?"

"You were so patient with me," I croaked, trying not to break down completely. "Didn't you ever get tired of those foolish questions?"

He let go my hand, and waived it as if he were dismissing me. "There are no foolish questions," he said. "Each encounter is fated; carefully chosen by your higher self. You sought me as I sought you."

"Please don't go," I sobbed.

"You know the drill, Brother Toby. Just close

your eyes and I'll be there." He closed his eyes then, and took a deep breath, like he used to do when I had asked a vexing question.

Soon enough he opened his eyes. "Come still closer, both of you."

We leaned in, almost bumping our heads to be closer. He raised both hands, and rapped both of us on the forehead with two fingers crossed.

A jolt of power surged through me, and I gasped. My mind flooded with brilliant rainbow colors, which raced up and down my spine. It was as if an internal cyclone had struck. It was all I could do to simply try to breathe and stay on my feet, so intense was the feeling.

Just for a second I glanced at Truong, and he was having as hard a time with it as I was. We actually bumped together, and bounced apart. Surges of power coursed through me. Muscles twitched and jumped. I began to hear strange music, sort of like a chorus of hums and horns and flutes.

I began to laugh, and noticed that Truong was laughing too. We laughed and laughed and the Abbot sat up in bed and laughed with us. And the laughter turned to tears, and then we three cried out of pure joy. And soon enough it faded and all was quiet. The Abbot folded his hands in a silent blessing. "And now," he whispered, "my work is finished."

His eyes fluttered shut and once again he

became old and tired and pale. He inhaled sharply, and let it out. And I felt his spirit leave the room. Truong's eyes met mine. He shook his head and shrugged. I was totally exhausted and totally at peace.

"What are we supposed to do now?" Truong asked.

I felt my mouth opening, and I felt myself saying words that I had not thought. It was as if I was being lived by someone else. The voice I recognized as belonging to Brother Toby said. "We are to follow the path, of course."

We left the room and walked in silence through the darkened hallway. The old doctor bowed as we passed. I was no longer sad, nor tired, nor happy. Just empty.

Preparations for the funeral kept all of us busy for four days. Monks and nuns began to arrive from all over Southeast Asia. The Abbot's body lay on a white marble slab. Although he was not given any embalming fluid his body did not seem to disintegrate. Many of the monks came by to visit with me, laugh, and talk to me about my great "escape." The Abbot had told them that I was preparing, and suggested to each of them what they might offer as a gift. They all had so much fun with it, and had all hid in a nearby room and watched me as I made my way out the side door. They thought it was great fun.

Many were worried about my trip to Saigon, and

offered advice and contacts for me to seek out. I heard each one, and tried to remember, but was not willing to take the chance and write down any names. I figured that if I were caught, then any contact I had would be endangered.

As the funeral date got closer, my mood darkened. I had been so sure of myself while I knew he was alive. I was sure I was destined to be a Buddhist monk. I thought I knew that I was destined to lecture and learn and practice the path of loving-kindness.

But now the sureness was gone. I had always thought he would be around to talk to, ask questions of. Now he was gone.

My mood got darker and blacker, and I finally told Truong that I could not go to the funeral. He asked me if I was sure I wanted to miss it. I nodded, and he left.

I stayed in my room for a week. I hardly ate at all, and never went to lecture or service. I had no visitors. I could hear the gong of the prayer call, and the chanting of the monks. But I couldn't will myself to move. For the first time in my life, I thought of suicide.

In my unit, lots of guys thought of suicide. One guy actually did it. He just walked outside of camp, far enough away so that he wouldn't hurt anyone else. He sat down near an outcropping of rocks and pulled the pin on a grenade.

All of us thought the camp was under attack, but

one of his squad mates came and told me that he capped himself. "He was tired of it all," was all he said.

There had been a lot of guys that had those kinds of feelings, and I had done my best to talk to them. I had been so sure that I could never even think like that.

Everyone could tell when someone had given up. He would give all of his things to his buddies, and maybe even write letters and ask friends to make sure they got delivered. Sometimes they didn't actually kill themselves, they just stopped being careful. They would just do something stupid and die. I would shake my head and say I could never do that. And here I was, not sure if I should live or die.

Wasn't I supposed to have died in the jungle? Now the war was over, or nearly over, and I could hitch rides with the North Vietnamese Army, and not even worry. And yet I couldn't think of even one reason why I should live another day.

A sound at the door let me know that someone was bringing me food. I waited until I was sure they were gone, and opened the door. There was a bowl of rice soup and a cup of tea.

I looked at the food. I had absolutely no sense of hunger, no desire to eat or drink anything. I finally got into bed and pulled the cover over my head and closed my eyes. A cloud of darkness enveloped my mind and I shivered and curled up into a ball.

I must have finally drifted off to sleep, because I came awake in the pitch dark with an urgent need to drain my bladder. I swung my feet to the floor and kicked the soup, sending it splattering out in front of me. "Shit!" I muttered.

I had to take small steps to keep from slipping in the rice soup, but managed to get the door open. The rain had come with a vengeance, and I muttered a curse and stepped to go out, but tripped over something in the doorway and lurched into a wall. Someone grabbed me and I swung wildly with my right fist. I connected against someone or something and heard a muffled cry and "So sorry!"

Now lights began to appear, and shadows moved in the courtyard. The roar of the rain was so intense that my brain could not seem to form even a single thought. I stood there in the doorway with my arms up in a boxer's pose.

The lights came closer, and I was able to make out a crumpled form at my feet. I knelt down and saw that it was Truong. A growing pool of black liquid came into focus, spreading out and away from his forehead.

I scooped him up in my arms like a child, and swung around back into my room. I found the bed and placed him on it. "Please bring a lantern!" I called.

My hand went to Truong's forehead, trying to stop the flow of blood, A monk appeared with a rag, and gently removed my hand and placed the rag of the wound.

I had hit him squarely in the forehead, above the eyes and below where the hairline would have been if he didn't shave his head. Right above the eyes was a deep gash, about an inch and a half long.

Someone else entered the room and removed the cloth and placed a large green leaf on the wound. I grabbed the rag and used it to clean up the pool of blood in the doorway.

Another monk with another rag appeared, and I took it and handed the blood soaked one. I opened my mouth to start to explain what happened, but no words came out. There just didn't seem any thinking going on in my brain tonight.

The roar of the rain was too loud to explain anything anyway. So I just closed my mouth and sat down and started to shiver. I closed my eyes to shut out the awful scene.

After a moment, I heard the Abbot's voice. It was from a lecture back at the other monastery. "When the mind is too agitated to meditate, simply listen to the breath. Notice breath going in, notice the hold, and then notice breath going out."

I sat all night on the floor, using my pillow as a meditation cushion. Dark and ominous shadows crept near me, bringing a fear to my throat that I could taste. Strange screams sounded in my head, and the doors rattled and shook like demons were trying to break down the door. I kept refocusing my mind as the Abbot had instructed, breathe in, hold, and breathe out.

Just before dawn, a small point of light appeared to my inner vision. It looked at first like a distant star in the blackest sky. But it moved closer, and grew in brilliance until it flooded the room. I was so sure I was dreaming that I opened my eyes, and was startled to see the entire room and the entire outside was flooded with a brilliant light.

All the fear and all the anger and frustration and hopelessness was lifted out of me by that light. And with each inward breath I could feel the light filling me with loving-kindness and compassion and trust. Beloved Abbot's voice spoke to my mind, and told me that I had gone through the darkness and out the other side. "Never again will you need to worry. Just trust the path, Master Toby."

"I smiled and remembered Honored Sir, the guy I had renamed because I couldn't say the name Phuoc with a straight face. The night of Truong's visit, he had insisted on calling me "Master Toby."

I stood and stretched at the first sound of the gong, and shuffled down the hall to the Temple area. The place was filling with monks and nuns. For some reason many of the monks stopped and bowed deeply when they saw me. I figured it was because I hadn't been present for the funeral, and they thought I had gone. I took a seat near the rear of the temple, in case I got bored with whoever was going to conduct the services.

I was sitting with my eyes closed when I felt a hand on my shoulder. I opened my eyes to see the old physician. "Brother Toby, would you please come with me?"

I stood and bowed and followed him, and he led me right up to the front of the temple, to a gold pillow exactly like the one the Abbot had used. He motioned for me to sit, and the room quieted as I did.

The old physician announced in a booming voice, "Brother Toby will conduct the lecture and prayers today. Offer him your fullest attention."

My mouth must have dropped, because I had no idea what this was all about. A sea of faces sat in anticipation. For a second, I panicked.

"Ask within to have the spirit of loving-kindness speak through you, and then sit a side and listen and learn," The Abbot's voice was still in residence in my mind. I remembered thinking I must be losing my mind.

No sooner did that thought occur than I heard the Abbot's voice again, "You cannot lose what you never had. Remember that you are not a thinker but merely a receptor. Either fear speaks through you, or loving-kindness does.

There are no neutral thoughts."

In the third row, I spotted the smiling face of

Truong, so I stood up and motioned him to the front. If I was going to make a fool of myself, then he could surely join me.

He came reluctantly, and I heard my voice announce that I would speak for the first part of the lecture, and then Master Truong would continue.

He looked at me and mouthed the word "Master?" I just nodded and smiled.

The lecture was about right seeing, and it was great. The Abbot spoke through me for at least an hour before I heard myself announcing that I was leaving this very afternoon for Saigon, and that Master Truong was the chosen monk to continue with the Beloved Abbot's teachings.

All of the monks and all of the nuns stood and clasped their hands in a reverent bow as I left. By sunset I was back in Viet Nam, and on the road to Saigon. My step was sure and strong, and my heart was filled with peace.

Chapter 10

My backpack was stuffed with food of all kinds. The monks and I had calculated that it was over five hundred miles to Saigon, and they must have decided to pack enough food for that distance. The pack was so heavy that I struggled each time I put it on or took it off.

Although the river was the shortest distance, I was told to avoid it at all costs. The last vestiges of resistance by the Southern forces were along the river, and there was a much higher possibility of a firefight or an ambush if I traveled that way. And so I set out to follow the Ho Chi Minh Trail.

Since the withdrawal of American forces, the trail had gone public. No longer was it necessary to travel only at night, and no longer was it necessary to switch from branch to branch on the trail. Nowadays, a steady stream of trucks and artillery equipment and tanks rumbled down that trail.

I was walking along the path leading from the Mekong River to the trail, and encountered two young soldiers going the same direction. They had been going faster than I was able to, and I hailed them as they came alongside.

"I have too much food. Would you please honor me by joining me for a meal and helping to lighten my pack?"

They were delighted to accept the offer, and they proved up to the task by consuming enough food to last me for a week. I kept feeding them until they finally told me they could eat no more.

During dinner, we introduced ourselves. The older of the brothers was named Binh, and his younger brother was Pham. They were heading south to join up with their cousin, who had journeyed to Saigon to help with the revolution.

Binh was the more reserved of the two, and after the introductions his brother did most of the talking. They didn't seem to mind at all that I was an American, and even showed me pictures of their children.

"Please bless these pictures," Pham said. "We are probably not going to see them until the war ends."

So I blessed the pictures. Pham had two daughters, ten months apart. They both looked as if they had been stamped from a production mold. One seemed to be just a younger picture of the older one. When I commented on their beauty, He assured me that their mother was the most beautiful woman in the village.

Bihn then showed me his picture. It was a black and white photo of a young boy, maybe ten months old. The face was sad and serious and enough like Pham's that I asked if this was not a picture of Pham as a young boy.

Both men laughed and Binh said, "Everyone who saw him said exactly the same thing!"

"Show us some pictures of your children," said Pham.

"I have no pictures because I have no children." I explained.

Both men tried to console me, although I tried in vain to convince them that I was not sure I was really ready for children.

We walked together the few miles that led to a huge staging area. There must have been hundreds of trucks parked alongside of each other. Tanker trucks methodically refueled each one in turn. Soldiers in uniform milled with the irregulars of the Viet Cong. The hot topic of the day was trying to predict the fall of Saigon.

Every once in a while an officer of the NVA would appear, and try to organize the chaos, but it never seemed to help. I was eager to be on the road, but not about to tell anyone my reasons.

Binh and Pham finally located a truck that was to leave in the morning, and talked the man in charge into hauling me with them.

Although the South Vietnamese had not surrendered, and often put up a stiff resistance, the soldiers all talked as if the war was over. I sat in the shade of a huge tree and tried to meditate, but found myself eavesdropping on the conversations all around.

Rumors flew like crazy, and after a while I decided to just be in the moment and see what came up. Soon enough, I was able to find a quiet center in my mind and rest in my meditation.

The night came, and soon enough the day. I stood up stiffly after sitting for the entire night, and Pham came running over.

"Brother Toby, come at once! We were waiting for the wrong truck. The one we want is leaving right away!"

I grabbed my pack and followed him across a field. A truck was backing up to get onto the road, and Binh waived and pounded on the roof of the truck until it stopped.

We clamored aboard, and it jerked and bumped off towards the south. I realized that I had been more concerned than I had let on. My neck and shoulders were stiff and sore. I consciously focused my mind to focus on the muscles around my shoulders and neck, and soon was so relaxed I nearly fell asleep.

We drove all that morning, and at the mid-day break I was invited to bless the meal and the soldiers. I was glad to do so, and felt like I was at least contributing something to earn my ride.

My companions were now fifteen young men and a gruff old sergeant type who took it upon himself to keep things right and tight. Apparently he would be the squad leader of this exuberant bunch once it reached the outskirts of Saigon.

His name turned out to be Mr. Dai. He objected to being called "old man" and chastised the youngsters for not showing their elders proper respect. Mr. Dai had been a soldier for over thirty years, and despite his gruffness, seemed to care a lot about these young men.

But he didn't care for me. He showed his displeasure when I was invited to bless the meals, or bless the photographs. Maybe he didn't like Buddhists, or maybe he was a Catholic, or maybe he recognized me as an American and had seen too many comrades die at the hands of Americans.

He pointedly refused to acknowledge me, and I quickly gave up trying to engage him in any conversation. But then, he was not the greatest conversationalist in the truck by a long shot. So I mostly rode in silence. Often I would meditate, or just doze. The young men amused themselves by singing.

Songs in Viet Nam don't need to rhyme, or have a certain cadence. They are usually stories or legends sung in a sing-songy voice that rises and falls in no apparent pattern. Usually one person would start the song, and get to a key idea, and repeat it sort of like the bridge of a song. Then someone else would join in, singing the bridge part and then adding their own part, telling something significant in their lives or recalling some great deed.

It wasn't unusual for one song to go on for several hours. It was sort of fun, and it helped the miles go by.

When the scenery shifted from lowlands to higher plateaus, I had the uncanny feeling that I had been here before and something awful was about to happen. I was startled to realize that I knew in advance that there would be a disabled truck, and a rice paddy with two women...and... and...

Suddenly I stood up and hollered, "Stop this truck!" I began to bang on the roof of the cab! "Stop here! There is a woman in great danger!"

Mr. Dai jumped up and chambered a round in his AK-47 and aimed it at my head. "Shut up and sit down now!" he ordered.

I turned to him. "You must get this truck to stop. There is a woman who is about to drown . And if she drowns, she will lose her first-born son ! Stop this truck!"

"Sit down now!" he screamed.

"Stop the truck! If this woman dies, it will be

your karma for life!" That got to him. He banged on the truck with me, and it jerked to a stop. The driver got out and wanted to know what was going on.

"A woman is about to die. We can save her," I shouted. "She is just over there!" I pointed off past a low hill.

Just then an old man appeared, waiving and shouting in the distance. Just as I knew he would, but I don't know how I knew it.

I jumped out of the bed of the truck and landed on my bad leg, collapsing in a heap in the dust. Pham jumped out too.

He pulled me to my feet. "Where?" he asked. "Which way?"

I ran as best as I could over the low hill and into a flooded rice paddy. Pham outran me and found a woman lying face down in the water. He was pulling on her arm when I slogged over and grabbed her around the waist and pulled her out of the water.

She was very pregnant, with a very large bulge in the belly. And she was not breathing.

Mr. Dai waived his weapon at me. Do something, monk! Or I will pull this trigger. Save her now!"

I dragged the lifeless woman to an area of high ground and rolled her over onto her belly. Then I grabbed her from the back and lifted her torso and squeezed with both arms. Her mouth opened and water streamed out. I squeezed again and she coughed and spewed more water and then screamed.

From somewhere behind me an old woman appeared. "Get away! Don't touch her!" she screamed. She grabbed the back of my robe and pulled me off my feet, dumping me butt first into the flooded field. I still had hold of the pregnant woman, who landed on top of me, still screaming.

The old woman managed to kick at me as I landed, still yelling for me to leave. Pham and Mr. Dai quickly made themselves scarce.

I managed to get to my feet, thoroughly soaked, and she turned on me again. "Go away! Just leave! Don't look at her!"

I avoided her flailing arms and beat a hasty retreat, catching up with Pham and Mr. Dai. We walked in silence back to the truck. Just as we were getting back into the bed of the truck we heard the squalling cries of a newborn baby.

Mr. Dai looked as white as a ghost. "How could you know?" he asked. I shrugged. I didn't know how I knew.

That infuriated Mr. Dai. He stood up in the moving truck, trying to level his weapon at me. Many hands reached out to try to stabilize him, and some pulled the gun down. "How could you know! How could you know!"

I opened my mouth but no words came. I shrugged again, and now he raised his voice even louder. The other young men in the truck gently grabbed him, afraid a sudden turn might throw him clear out. He reluctantly took his seat and lowered his weapon. To himself he muttered something I couldn't hear.

No one spoke for the rest of the ride that afternoon. When we stopped for evening meal, he avoided me, and was not even present when I blessed the meal.

Later he came and sat beside me. His face was tired and somehow older. He shook his head back and forth. Finally he spoke. "You can speak to ghosts, can't you?" All eyes in the camp were on me. I had no idea how to respond to that question, so I went quietly within. I was sure that the Abbot must have an answer. So I waited, and waited, and waited some more.

I could hear the ragged breathing of Mr. Dai. I could see the flickering fire as it danced and licked at the logs. I could actually hear the blood coursing through the veins and arteries in my head.

It got very still. I waited, but maybe the old Abbot was out to lunch, or maybe he was sleeping, or meditating or playing a harp in heaven. He sure was somewhere else.

I shook my head, "No. I am sorry I cannot explain what happened. I knew because I may have dreamed about it, or seen it in a meditation. I really don't know how I knew."

He looked at me with no expression whatsoever.

"I only know that I knew." I repeated.

The old soldier nodded, like he understood. I started again. "I had dreamed earlier of that entire scene. I knew the turns in the road, the shape of the trees, and that low hill. I knew an old man would come running." He nodded.

"And I knew that if we didn't save her, she and her child would have died."

We finished our meal in silence, and almost immediately the soldiers were preparing to bed down. There was no singing, no bragging and no talk at all. I sat in the lotus position and let my eyes close.

I thought of the woman, and the anger of Mr. Dai. I remembered the black mood that overtook me at the time of the Abbot's passing, and I recalled that I had asked why I should go on living. Now I knew. And then just when I didn't need it, the old Abbot's soft voice appeared in my mind. It was from a question I had asked long ago. "Each of us comes to this life with a mission. Many of us spend years not knowing our purpose. Yet our mission is always the same; to serve all of our brothers and sisters, and all living beings. When we accept that mission we live under the light of harmony. Everything that we try to do seems to work. Not for our own desires, but for the good of all."

So I sat there, not tired, not needing sleep. I sat there and went to that place in the mind where thinking slowed. I watched as thoughts flitted up and into my awareness; thoughts that I noted without attachment. They lingered for an instant, and then they faded, only to be replaced by another.

Soon the thoughts didn't even bother to arise. What was left? What was left was a sense of indescribable joy; a joy so intense my eyes couldn't contain the tears of gratitude, and so they cascaded down my face and into my lap.

A hand softly touched me on the shoulder. "Gentle monk, the truck is about to leave. Are you riding further with us?"

It was Mr. Dai. I looked around and saw that the camp had been cleared. Only Mr. Dai and Pham and Binh were still on the ground. The others were sitting in their places on the truck bed.

I tried to stand, but my legs were numb. Mr. Dai and Pham grabbed me just before I fell on my face. With one man on each side, they actually lifted me and set me on the rolled up canvass that had become my seat of preference.

Binh was the last one aboard, and he latched the tailgate and we roared off to the south.

My bowl, filled with hot tea, miraculously appeared in my hand, passed by one of the young men. Only a small amount had been spilled, and that tea tasted as good as any I can recall.

For the next ten hours we journeyed south, part of a huge convoy of trucks and men and equipment. From time to time someone would hand me a photograph, and ask me to bless it. Many times it was of parents, or children or siblings left behind, but occasionally I would see one that showed a young man or woman of military age.

"Is my cousin still amongst us?" they would ask.

I would look at the face in the photograph, and I would know. Sometimes I could tell them yes, they are fine. Other times I would shake my head and offer a silent prayer that their soul would be at peace.

The young men in the truck would nod, and cast their eyes down for a moment, and thank me. I have no way of knowing if I was correct, but got used to the sense of clarity that I would feel when I looked at a picture. Mr. Dai, who sat beside me, would say, "He doesn't know how he knows, but he knows he knows." And the young men would nod and put away the pictures.

At dusk the next day, we came to another huge clearing. It was filled with vehicles of all sorts. I saw armored personnel carriers made in America, I saw Soviet light tanks, Chinese jeeps with 50 caliber machine guns mounted on the front and rear. But mostly I saw troop trucks like the one I had ridden. There were hundreds and hundreds of them, almost too many to count.

I thought of the ARVN troops, if there were any of them still capable of resisting the NVA. Silently, I prayed for a peaceful end to the killings.

Pham and Binh approached and offered me gifts,

brown cloth sacks of food. "Brother Toby," Pham said. "My brother and I thank you for your blessings and your gifts of friendship. We are leaving for our battle assignments, and wished for one more blessing." Both bowed deeply and I placed my hands on their heads, just as the Abbot had done to me. They turned to leave, but Binh came back.

"Brother Toby, be careful. We are at the place where Cambodia and Viet Nam intersect. If you wander into Cambodia by mistake, you will be killed. We are hearing of thousands of monks and nuns being slaughtered." His brother added, "May you be abundantly blessed in your journey. "

I watched them walk away. I remembered the lecture of the old Abbot about rising above wanting and not wanting. He taught me a prayer, and laughed as he explained it to me. "When you pray this prayer, "he said, "it is always instantly granted. Here is the prayer. Let all things be exactly as they are!"

After he told me that prayer, he giggled and clapped his hands. "If you can remember that prayer, you shall never know unhappiness." I remembered looking at him like he must be crazy.

"Think about it, Brother Toby. All suffering comes from wanting and not wanting, so if you can let all things be the way they are, you have transcended suffering."

I thanked them both for their kind advice and asked them to point the path that I should take to get over the hill to the village of Quan Loi. My map showed it to be the quickest way to Saigon. They warned me again about not getting lost and ending up in Cambodia. One more blessing and they were gone.

I thought about that prayer as I watched the two brothers walk away. At some level, I knew neither one would survive their first battle. Again, I heard my Abbot's voice, "Let all things be exactly as they are, Brother Toby." Easy to say, hard to do, I thought.

Chapter 11

The trail was flat for about an hour, and then inclined upward. I tried to keep a good pace, but found myself slowing down as the hills seemed to get higher. For most of the morning, I climbed. The foliage got thicker and the trees seemed taller. I found myself in the shade most of the time.

Tall trees and huge meadows of elephant grass filled the landscape. The path became much steeper, and the constant climbing slowed my progress. The path also became less defined, and often I would wander down what I thought was the main trail, to find that it rejoined a larger trail. The canopy of trees was so thick that I couldn't see the sun, and could not verify what direction I was moving.

My foot started to hurt again, and I found myself pausing often. It occurred to me that this way may be the shortest distance on a map, but it certainly was not the easiest path to walk. Finally, I crested a mountaintop and paused to look down the path that stretched ahead. Was that a river?

I took my backpack off and sat down, rummaging to find the map. I could not recall seeing a river on the map, but it sure looked like one was right below me. I wished for good pair of binoculars. Almost immediately the words of the Abbot sprang up inside my head. "Wishing is a form of rejection of what is. To wish it were different is to refuse to accept how it is." So I accepted that I didn't have a pair of binoculars. Reluctantly.

I searched again, but couldn't find the map. And I couldn't even recall the last time I had looked at it, so I carefully removed everything from the pack. A third and thorough search showed me that the map was gone. I wondered if someone might have taken it during one of my naps on the truck. Anyway, I had no map.

Once again that prayer popped into my mind. "Let all things be exactly as they are." The reality of the moment was that I didn't have the map. I decided my only choice was to be okay with not having it, or being upset. Knowing I had a choice made it easy to decide not to be upset about the map.

I stood up and started off down the hill. Beloved Abbot's voice softly said, "It is much easier to choose peace when we are aware of choices, eh, Brother Toby?"

I liked his logic, but didn't approve of his timing. I headed down the path, hoping to find a decent place to make a camp. The hour was getting late, and the rumbling in my stomach said it was nearing dinnertime. I found a small stream, and decided that it would probably be the fastest route to the river, so I left the trail and followed the stream. The only problem with my plan is that the stream quickly turned into a small river with steep banks and rapids. My plan had been to walk alongside the small stream, but as it descended, it grew, and the canyons it traversed often had steep walls.

I found myself having to wade in the chilly water occasionally. As darkness descended, I located a sandbar at a turn in the stream that had become a river. I sat down and ate some cold rice and vegetables. I wanted some tea, but didn't want to wait for the water to boil, so I hefted my pack and continued to slosh down towards the base of the mountain.

I rounded a bend in the stream and came upon the intersection of the stream and a wider river. Out in the middle of the watercourse was a small sandy island with some bamboo and shrubbery. I decided that it would make good sense to spend the night there, so I waded the short distance to the island.

I found a spot that seemed hidden behind a larger tree. Low bushes fanned out in nearly a complete circle around the tree, affording me a windbreak and a place to hide out of sight. Within minutes, I had a fire and was heating a pot of water for tea.

The water took a long time to boil, and darkness fell quickly. By the time I could hear the soft hissing of the teapot, I couldn't see much of anything.

I sipped the green tea in total darkness. A small package of sticky rice was wrapped in cabbage leaves, and I gratefully and slowly consumed it. I leaned back against the trunk of the tree and fell asleep.

Something awakened me in the pitch-black night! I wasn't sure if it was a noise, or a premonition. I was sure that I was fully alert, wide awake, and certain that I had cause for concern.

I held my breath and listened. The night was suddenly silent. No sounds of bugs, no critters scurrying in the dark. I focused my senses, listening for the slightest footfall, hoping to hear the snap of a twig.

I waited with my heart pounding, trying in vain to peer into the darkest shadows. A flood of sensations I hadn't experienced in a long time reminded me of my life on patrol. The difference is that now I had no weapon. Not even the K-bar knife. I sat there, nearly immobilized, listening with all my might, trying to pick up some sign of danger. My breath was short and shallow. After a long silence I decided that maybe I was just getting spooky, so I forced myself to relax and breathe deep and regularly. I did try, however not to breathe noisily.

Suddenly an arm came around my neck. Out of the dark shadows I could see the shapes of men. A knife was pressed against my neck, but it was so dull it just served to cut off my breath.

One by one, five shadowy figures materialized around me. By their silhouettes I at first thought they were longhaired women, but their terrible body odors told me that I was encountering the soldiers of Cambodia. The grip on my neck and the knife were removed as the person behind the tree came around front. I just sat there, sure that any sudden move would be my last.

A face came closer and closer to my face, and I thought the man was going to kiss me, he came so close. Something was said in a language I didn't understand. I nearly gagged at the smell of his breath. When I remained silent, it was said louder. I said in Vietnamese that I did not understand, and was struck on the side of my head, probably by a rifle butt.

The blow nearly knocked me unconscious, but it sure knocked me over on my side. Soon a kick landed in my midsection. I exhaled in pain, curled up in a ball, and covered my head.

I heard the clack of a rifle chambering a round, and heard also a voice give an order. It must have been the Cambodian word for "Stop!"

My eyes were adjusted to the darkness, or else dawn was approaching, because I could dimly make out the features of six men. The one who had ordered the beating to end now said in Vietnamese, "You are a very stupid monk, monk!"

I could see that he held an ancient Enfield carbine, a weapon from the first world-war era. The others had backed away, and he was holding the weapon pointed not so much at me, as the entire group.

"What is your name, monk?" said the man with the rifle.

Now I knew that my Abbott had stressed the need to tell the truth, but I made a command decision that if I mentioned I was an American, my life span would be milliseconds, not years. So I lied.

"I am known as Brother Truong, I am on my way to the village of Quin Loi."

The rifleman laughed without any humor. "You are very lost then, this island is claimed by both Cambodia and Viet Nam. Quin Loi is over that mountain."

I didn't have to turn and look to know it was the same mountain I had descended earlier.

"I am sorry for intruding. May I offer you food? I have food to share."

"You have nothing!" he said. "We now have the pack and we now have the food. We have no intention of sharing it with a foolish Buddhist! We have the power to end your life right now. We shoot all trespassers into Cambodia."

"But you said yourself that this island is disputed, is the life of a confused monk necessary to protect your country?" There was enough light that I could see his face, and he actually smiled briefly.

"Go now!" he said. "They can't understand Vietnamese, and I will keep them from killing you. A monk once saved my life, and so I am sparing yours. Climb that stream bank and make sure you never come near the Mekong again."

I scrambled to my feet. The others jumped and one produced a huge machete. The man with the rifle barked an order and pointed the gun at the machete man. A surly response I couldn't understand followed, but he lowered the machete. In Vietnamese the man said again "Go now!"

I didn't need any more encouragement, so I just waded into the river and retraced my steps to the mouth of the smaller stream. I scrambled up the bank and began pulling myself hand over hand up the steep watercourse. I looked back to see all six of them standing and watching my progress. I was tempted to bow, but thought better of it.

I kept moving until the sun was up, and I was up at a much higher elevation. I finally rested where I could see the river far below. I was cold and hungry. Even in the tropics, there is a time just after sunrise when the temperature drops rapidly. My robe was wet from wading, and I was exhausted. But I was still within sight of Cambodia, and had no desire to encounter any marauding bands. I forced myself to stand and continue to climb.

I still had the problem of being lost, and wasn't sure how I was going to find the path or the trail to Qin Loi. But I decided that right now I had better put some distance between me and that river.

I walked all morning, and near the noon hour I crested the summit. Just briefly, I thought I saw someone or something following me, so I rounded a bend and quickly hid myself behind a gnarled and misshapen tree. I had no weapon, no food, and no clue what I would do if someone was following me. The best I could do was to just stay hidden and let whoever it was pass.

Within minutes I saw him. It was the guy with the rifle. He was busy studying the trail and he followed it right up to the point where I stepped off to hide behind the tree. He stood and looked at the tree. "Monk! You can come out. I am not going to hurt you!"

I hesitated, and he put the rifle on the ground and stepped back about six or seven paces. "I wish to become a monk! I have tired of the killings.

Please help me."

I stepped around to the front of the tree. "Where are your comrades?" He bowed and motioned toward the old rifle. "Please take it. I have renounced violence. I shall never touch a weapon again."

I asked again, "And where are your comrades?"

"They are not my comrades,' he said. "In Cambodia all men are organized into cadres of seven, and ordered to search out and kill the enemies of the state."

I looked at the weapon, and looked down the trail the way we had both come. He shook his head, "They remain in Cambodia, or on that island. Enough people make the mistake you made, and they kill them for their food or clothes. I cannot continue."

"Won't they come after you, or us?" I asked.

Again he shook his head. "They are lazy and have no desire to intrude too deeply into Viet Nam. There is talk of Viet Nam sending soldiers to stop the Cambodians from raiding."

I studied the old rifle. "I don't want it, but you may."

He followed my gaze, and shook his head. "I have killed my last man. I have no use for it either. Shall I put it in the river?"

I nodded, and he emptied the shells and flung each in a different direction, and then removed the bolt action and flung it deeply into the trees, away from the river. The remaining part of the gun he took to the nearby stream. I watched as he knelt and scooped the mud deep enough to bury the weapon. He then found two boulders and placed them on the spot. Satisfied, he smiled and returned to the path. "Now I am a Buddhist," he proclaimed.

"You still look like a Cambodian raider," I said with a smile, "And you smell like one too."

A smile spread across his face, and he bowed. "I am to assume that my teacher uses sarcasm as one of his teaching devices. Please wait while I bathe." With that he strode to the stream and stripped his clothes. He had no soap, and the stream must have been cold, but he managed to scrub with the sand. He used his shirt to towel with.

I smiled and said, "The hair is still a dead give-away."

"Ah!" he said. "The hair. Well, yes." He produced a knife that he carefully sharpened by honing it on a boulder. When it finally met his approval he grabbed his long hair and hacked it off in huge chunks. After several minutes he looked like a half-skinned skunk.

"Let me have that blade," I said. I took it and carefully shaved the clumps of missed hair. It was surprisingly sharp, although it left his scalp mottled and blotchy. The lack of hair also revealed a snow-white scalp.

"That will have to do. We must find a monastery, and get you a saffron robe." I returned the knife and

untitled

motioned for him to begin walking, and we proceeded to a clearing, with a fork in the path.

"That road," he said, pointing to a barely discernible path, "leads right back to Cambodia. And this one, is the road to Quin Loi."

"I don't suppose you brought any of my food, did you?"

He shook his head. "They were insistent that if I left, I leave the food. I didn't feel like killing any of them, so I left it for them. Buddhists refrain from killing, right?"

I nodded, trying not to show my disappointment. And that lead right into the lecture of the Four Noble Truths, the first of which dealt with suffering. We walked and talked, or rather he talked and I listened.

"My mother was Cambodian, but my father was Vietnamese. He insisted I learn both languages. He tried to talk to me about the eight-fold path, and the middle way of the Buddha, but I was young and impertinent."

"He will be proud of you for your decision to return to your roots."

He shook his head. Tears welled up in his eyes and he stopped walking. I waited in silence.

"I was present when both of my parents were killed." His voice wavered, "Roving squads were pointing out anyone who could read or write. I might have been able to save them, but I feared disapproval of the cadre commander. He later told me that my duty to the Khymer Rouge led me to choose rightly to denounce them."

I didn't know what to say. So I just nodded. He looked at me with such bleakness and pain and I had no words to comfort him. I took a deep breath, and the voice of my Abbot spoke.

"Tell him of your adventure in the tunnel, and the being of light. Tell him what the being said about your commandment."

And so I told him that although all intelligent humans eventually forsake violence, that I had died, and visited a being of light. He asked me how I died, and why I was still here, and I had to relay the whole story.

The day passed, and he foraged for food and found wild vegetables to feed us. We talked late into the night, and he took great comfort from my story. In the morning he asked, "How can I undo the horrible karma I have taken on?"

Since I had asked the Abbot the exact same question, I was able to recall almost word for word the answer I was given.

"We are ruled by the laws of karma as long as we believe in the concept of "self and other." The law of Grace transcends the law of karma, and is easily understood when we cease to see the world as "self and other" and begin to see it as "self as other."

That concept elicited many more questions, but

at some deep level I was able to convince him that the essence of us is eternal, unchanging, and incapable of being killed. I was impressed by his thirst for answers, and delighted to share the things I had learned.

We rounded a bend and saw black smoke and plumes of flames. Several huts were perched on poles around a barren hill that served as the common ground of a village. Three of the huts were badly damaged and two were smoldering.

An old woman sat in the middle of the path, crying and tearing at her hair.

She sobbed and rocked back and forth. When she saw us she stopped, mid sob, and jumped to her feet. She pointed a bony and misshapen hand at us and screamed "Murderers! Murderers! You killed them all!"

I stood there in front of her until she finally stopped screaming. "Are you hurt?" I asked.

"Dead!" she screamed. "They're all dead! You and your filthy soldiers killed them all!"

"I am a monk," I said. "I didn't kill them. I just arrived and heard your cries." She spit right in my eyes. "Murderer!" My compatriot just stood there. I guess he was sure that this happened all the time to me, and I knew exactly how to handle it. The old woman noticed him standing there, and included him in her wrath. "Filthy bastards! You are all murderers! My whole family is dead! Have you no heart?"

She lunged suddenly at my throat, her arms outstretched to choke me. I stepped backwards, and tripped, and she landed fully on top of me. I managed to trap her hands and keep her from my neck, but she was writhing and struggling.

My companion grabbed her and easily pulled her off me. I let go and he deposited her back on her feet. I got to my feet and dusted off my robe and my dignity. "Who did this?" I asked, waiving at the carnage.

"Soldiers," she said in a surprisingly calm voice. "Cambodians?" I asked.

She looked hard at me. I was almost sure she saw me as a long-nose, an intruding American invader.

"What does it matter? Everyone who comes here comes only to murder. Now I am old and alone. My husband is dead. My sons are gone to war or dead. My daughters have fled to Saigon, and become whores!"

I didn't know what to tell her to comfort her. I waited, hoping the voice of the Abbot would help me, but there was only silence. I glanced around and saw several bodies.

"The dead must be buried. Can you find me some digging tools?" I went to the nearest hut. A young boy lay face down in the doorway. I saw at least four bullet holes in his small body. He was maybe eight or ten years old. I picked up the body and carried it to the old woman. "Do you have a burial site?"

She studied the body for a moment and then marched around to the back of one of the huts. My new student appeared carrying the body of an old man, probably the woman's husband. We carefully laid the bodies down on the damp earth.

The old woman watched us for an instant before turning and walking away. I knelt down on my hands and knees and started scooping the dirt away with my hands. The Cambodian did the same.

The old woman reappeared with two U.S Army issue folding foxhole shovels. She handed one to each of us. I thanked her and dug a decent grave for the boy, placed him in it and then helped with the digging for the old man. The woman stood and watched.

We found four more bodies, and the entire day was spent digging graves. I conducted a simple Buddhist ceremony, asking that the souls went quickly to heaven and only their good karma was recorded.

The old woman went inside one of the huts. I turned to my new friend and said, "I never asked you your name, nor told you mine. I am Brother Toby."

He bowed. "I am honored to have you as a teacher, Brother Toby. I am known as Lam."

The woman reappeared with two cups of tea, handing one to each of us.

"Do you have any for yourself?" I asked. She

shook her head. "You dug the graves. You drink the tea."

I shook my head, and offered the tea back to her. "You lost your entire family. Could we perhaps share it?"

She drew in a deep breath. "You are a strange monk." She pointed at the Cambodian, "And he does not even wear a robe. Who is he?"

Again I pushed the cup closer to her. "He is a new acolyte. And you are a strong and brave woman who has suffered much. Please drink the tea."

She took the cup and sipped. She closed her eyes and allowed the liquid to warm her. Then she opened her eyes and handed the cup back to me. "I have had all I want. I have something I must do." She bowed and said, "Goodnight, strange monk and stranger acolyte."

I watched her enter a nearby hut and close the door.

Lam and I sat down on the rough ground, and I taught him the method of observing his breath. Darkness came, and I ended the lesson. He stood and yawned, then stretched and lay down. "Goodnight, Brother Toby, who introduced himself yesterday as Brother Truong." He smiled and closed his eyes.

I sat the entire night. I slowed my mind to the place where no thoughts arose. A deep sense of peace engulfed me. Sometime during the night I must have dozed.

I was awakened by the crackle of flames and the acrid odor of burning straw. The old woman was systematically torching each of the huts. When she finished, she came to me and bowed. "I now have nothing and am a follower of the Buddha. I sit at your feet and await your instruction."

Lam smiled and produced his trusty knife, "All Buddhists shave their heads," he said. She nodded and began hacking her hair away. He watched in silence until she handed back the knife and stood silently as he finished the shaving.

I closed my eyes in order to become a silent observer of my sinking emotions. Desperation engulfed me as I called on the spirit of the Abbot. "Help!" I prayed silently.

Immediately, I heard his cosmic chuckle. "When the teacher is ready, the students will appear."

13639876R10129

Made in the USA
San Bernardino, CA
22 December 2018